SHE HAS BEEN CHOSEN.

A union of unspeakable terror awaits her—
and there are only a few trusted compan-
ions she can turn to—

her best friend

her doctor

her psychic

her lover.

But one of them is already possessed by the
dark sexual demon, Astragoth. To choose
wrongly will damn her—and doom her
young son....

Fawcett Gold Medal Books
by Gary Brandner:

☐ HELLBORN   14414 $2.50

☐ THE HOWLING   13824 $2.50

☐ THE HOWLING II   14091 $1.95

HELLBORN

by

Gary Brandner

FAWCETT GOLD MEDAL • NEW YORK

HELLBORN

Copyright © 1981 Gary Brandner

Published by Fawcett Gold Medal Books, a unit of CBS Publications, the Consumer Publishing Division of CBS Inc.

ISBN: 0-449-14414-3

Printed in the United States of America

First Fawcett Gold Medal printing: July 1981

10 9 8 7 6 5 4 3 2 1

The Legend of Astragoth

In a time before men measured years, in a village of a distant land, the people in their ignorance committed a terrible sin. From the pages of the forbidden *Book of the Damned* they took the obscene ritual that called up the demon Astragoth. Thinking they had found a powerful servant, the foolish people soon learned that they were the captives of the demon. He took as tribute the most succulent of the lambs and piglets, the ripest of the grain, the choicest of the fruits, and the headiest of the village's wine. His only promise in return was that he would not destroy them. Well aware of the demon's power, the people dared not defy him.

The village lived for years with this unequal bargain until Astragoth made one more dreadful demand. He would have the beauteous village maiden Delphine as his bride. Even in those times when there were few laws and demons walked the earth, the idea of such a union was monstrous. For the first time since they had summoned him, the villagers resisted the demon. Astragoth showed his anger by ripping the arms from a helpless child, and the rebellion quickly collapsed.

Following the orders of the demon, the villagers burned the outline of a pentagram into the soil and led the silent Delphine into the center of the figure. They then withdrew hastily to observe from a safer distance.

As always, the appearance of the demon was preceded by a foul odor, a combination of rotting flesh, feces, and sulfur. The circle of villagers shrank back even farther. They averted their eyes, reluctant to look directly at the loathsome creature. Delphine alone faced Astragoth without flinching. She stood erect and saw unspeakable lust in the deep-red glow of the demon's eyes. With a growl, he approached to claim his bride.

Moments before Astragoth could possess the maiden there was a commotion among the villagers. They parted to allow an old man to pass through. He made his way without hesitation to the pentagram.

"Stop this abomination!" the old man cried. His white beard was matted and dusty with travel, his skin wrinkled, his hands like brown claws. Yet his voice was strong, his eyes clear. His name was Zeban. He was a maker of magic summoned from a far corner of the land by Delphine's anguished father when no one in the village dared to defy Astragoth.

The demon stopped his advance toward the maiden and turned his fiery eyes on the old man. Delphine looked at him in astonishment.

"Be strong, child," the old man said to her. "Together we will defeat the hellborn and send it back to the darkness whence it came."

Astragoth gave a mighty roar and turned his fury full upon the magician. A blast of hell's heat singed the hair of onlookers standing well away from the pentagram. Zeban stood his ground and gave no sign that he felt it. The demon then knew he would not have the maiden without a battle.

For a day and a night they circled each other, the magician and the demon, within the walls of the pentagram. And always close behind Zeban was Delphine, willing her own strength into the body of the old man. Incantation matched curse; the noon sky grew dark and unearthly fires brightened the midnight.

The end came suddenly. When he saw he could not put down the magician, Astragoth thundered with rage and vanished. All that remained was the trace of his stench. From the bowels of the earth all those present heard the parting words of the demon: *"The girl is mine! I shall have her!"*

The aged magician, exhausted by the battle, slumped to the ground. Delphine rushed to his side and knelt there cradling his head in her lap.

"Old one, you have done what no man could do, you have vanquished the demon."

Zeban's eyelids fluttered open. He rolled his head painfully from side to side. "The danger remains. Never relax your vigilance, child. The demon will not go gently. As long as there somewhere remains a single copy of the accursed *Book of the Damned*, another fool may raise up Astragoth once more. You must be always on your guard. The demon is wily and powerful, but he is not invincible, as we have seen here. He may appear to you, or seem to appear, but without the ritual summons, he stays in the darkness. Pray every night of your life that no one calls him back."

Tears spilled from Delphine's eyes and dropped on the old man's cheeks. "My lord, without your magic I would be helpless."

"No, child," the old man whispered. "It was you, not I, who sent down Astragoth. It was your courage, your will. I was merely the instrument." A coughing spasm wracked his frail body. "Now the instrument is finished."

The old magician died then in the arms of the maiden.

And below, the demon waited....

1

Diana Cross hitched up her new pair of designer jeans and studied the effect. She was twenty-eight, and proud of having the same slim figure she'd had at eighteen. The fitted jeans, she decided, were worth the fifty dollars she had paid at Bullock's. She tied her caramel-colored hair back with a brown ribbon that matched her eyes, and pulled on a sweatshirt with *USC Athletic Department* lettered on the front. The shirt was one of the few things of Jerry's Diana had kept around since the divorce.

She walked through the living room, stepping over Matthew, who lay phone on the floor, chin in his hands, watching *Scooby-Doo* on television.

"We're going to leave in just about five minutes," she said.

"I'm all ready," Matt answered without looking away from the screen.

Diana continued into the bright little kitchen and took the bowl of potato salad from the refrigerator. She spooned out a dab and tasted it. Not as good as her mother's, she decided, but plenty good enough. She transferred the salad to a square Tupperware container and fitted it into the Styrofoam picnic box. She added the fried chicken bought last night at Colonel Sanders, deviled eggs, a jar of sweet pickles, liverwurst and pea-nut butter sandwiches, Pepsi for Matt, and a split of Paul Masson Chablis for her. It looked like a lot of food for the two of them, but Diana wanted to be sure there was enough.

It would be the first picnic for her and Matt alone. When she was still married to Jerry they had gone on a picnic every Memorial Day and Labor Day weekend. Everything was arranged with military precision—traffic and weather conditions verified, route carefully marked on the Auto Club map, timing planned down to the minute. Everybody had a checklist to follow. With Jerry nothing was ever left to chance. That was one of the reasons the marriage had ended after seven years.

Diana's way was different. She had decided only yes-terday afternoon to go on a picnic. She had gone out last night to pick up the makings for the potato salad and the other things. She had no specific destination in mind. Her idea was just to drive up the Angeles Crest Highway into the mountains until they came to a likely spot.

Matthew was not as enthusiastic as Diana would have liked, but since it was April and the Saturday cartoons were starting to show reruns, he consented to go along. Diana felt she had not spent enough time alone with her son, and she was determined that they would enjoy themselves today.

Things started going wrong early. Somewhere after leaving the Ventura Freeway Diana missed a turn and they spent an hour winding through the streets of Al-tadena and Sierre Madre.

"When are we going to be in the mountains?" Matt asked.

"This is a shortcut," Diana told him. By the time she found the Angeles Crest Highway they were both hot and hungry. Matt was complaining that cartoons were more fun, and Diana was thinking he might be right.

After climbing the mountain road for half an hour they came to a small clearing with two picnic tables.

"How's this?" Diana asked.

"Kind of skuzzy," was Matt's opinion.

"Well, it's good enough," Diana decided. She unloaded the picnic box and carried it from the car to one of the tables while Matt walked behind her moodily kicking pine cones.

The cold potato salad and the wine revived Diana's spirits. "Isn't it nice up here?" she said, trying for a rise out of Matthew. "See how clear the air is."

"Yeah." Matt raised his narrow shoulders in an exaggerated sigh. "Are we going home pretty soon?"

"We'll go home when I'm ready." Diana was immediately sorry for her sharp tone when Matthew looked at her with large hurt eyes. "Just enjoy the open air, dear. We'll be back in the city soon enough."

Matthew sat stoically trying to crush an empty Pepsi can with his small hands. Diana decided the picnic had not been such a hot idea. She simply did not have Jerry's knack for organizing things.

A chipmunk scampered out from its hiding place in the roots of a Douglas fir and perched on its haunches, watching the people with tiny bright eyes.

"Oh, Matt, look at that."

The sudden delight in her little boy's face at seeing the chipmunk made the whole trip worthwhile for Diana. Matt slid off the bench and started toward the little animal, and it skittered out of sight.

"Be patient," Diana said. "He'll come back."

In less than a minute the chipmunk reappeared, cocking its head on one side, then the other.

Matthew laughed happily. "Can I feed him, Mom?"

"All right, but don't try to get too close. Put some

crumbs down and move away so it will know you're not trying to hurt it."

Matt tore bits of bread from a sandwich and placed them carefully on the ground. He stepped back and waited with painful anticipation. For several seconds the chipmunk did not move; then, traveling in little darts, it approached the bread crumbs. It picked up the morsels in tiny paws and ate, chewing rapidly and keeping its eyes on the people. Matt gave his mother a delighted grin, then returned his attention to the chipmunk.

Diana packed the remains of the picnic back into the box and settled herself on the bench with a paper cup of wine to watch Matthew play with the chipmunk. She would have loved a cigarette, but out of respect for the fire danger season she had left them home. Smoking was a habit of her college days that she had resumed since her divorce.

There was a screech of rubber as a dusty pickup truck braked suddenly and wheeled off the road to park next to Diana's Pontiac. Two young men in faded Levi's got out and stood flanking the truck. One was heavy-bodied with lank blond hair. The other was lean and dark with eyes set too close together. They looked Diana over arrogantly, and she felt the muscles of her back tighten.

The two men popped open cans of Budweiser and grinned at Diana. "We in time for the food, honey?" the dark one asked.

Diana forced a smile. "You just missed it."

"Well now, ain't that a shame." The dark young man talked with the exaggerated country accent affected by CB radio buffs. "You hear that, Bear? You *hear* that? Lady here says we come too late for supper."

"What about dessert?" said the fat one called Bear.

"Lady must have some goodies in that box, wouldn't you say, Joker?"

"No dessert." Diana tried hard not to show the fear that was building up in her.

"Now that's downright unfriendly," Joker said. "You don't need to go to any trouble for us. We'd be right happy to share whatever you got. Ain't that a fact, Bear?"

"Why, hell yes. I know I'd be willing to share what I got here with the lady."

Both young men laughed and drank their beer, watching her. Diana glanced over at Matt. He had forgotten the chipmunk and was watching the two young men curiously.

Diana said, "I don't think this is funny, so let's cut it out, okay?"

Joker widened his eyes and looked at Bear in mock surprise. "Funny? I wasn't bein' funny. Was you bein' funny?"

"Hell no, not me."

Joker turned back and lifted his beer can toward Diana. "All we meant was we'd be happy to share our beer with you. Ain't that right, Bear?"

"That's right, that's gospel."

"What did you think we meant?"

Diana ignored the question. "Thanks for the beer, but no thanks," she said. "Come on, Matt, we're going."

Matthew looked uncertainly from his mother to the two men. "Right now?"

"Come *on*."

Diana carried the picnic box to the car and shoved it in on the side away from the pickup. The two men grinned at her.

"Sure is a pity you got to go so soon," said Joker.

"We got lots more beer in the truck," said Bear.

"We got lots more of everything."

"What have you got?" Matt asked, standing on tiptoe to see into the back of the pickup.

"Oh, you'd be surprised, kid," said Joker. They both laughed.

"Get in the car," Diana said. She slammed the door behind Matt, then went around and got in behind the wheel. The two men looked on with amusement.

Diana reached across and snapped down the lock button on Matt's door. "Fasten your seat belt," she said.

"What for?"

"Because I'm telling you to, that's what for."

Sulking, Matthew locked the buckle of his seat belt. Diana started the car and backed out onto the road. As she cranked the steering wheel around to head the car down the mountain she saw the two young men toss their beer cans away and climb into the cab of the pickup. She was angry at herself for reacting so strongly. They were probably just fooling around and didn't mean any harm. But then, they just might have been dangerous. There were, she admitted, some serious disadvantages in being a woman without a man.

She steered the car down the twisting mountain road, and Matt turned on the radio to hard-rocking KLOS. Diana turned the volume down, but did not complain about the music. There were patches of ground fog on the road, and she had to give her full attention to driving. It was, she thought, an odd time of day for fog, but she was unfamiliar with the mountains, and supposed it must be a local peculiarity.

The fog thickened, boiling gray-white up toward the car. Diana slowed to less than twenty miles an hour. The road was just two lanes wide, with heavy boulders on the right and a narrow shoulder on the left before a steep drop to the canyon floor. She turned on the headlights and the windshield wipers, but they were

14

little help as she leaned forward and peered into the murk.

Along with the fog came an odor so foul it made her gag. Diana's first thought was that there must be a sulfur spring nearby, but there was something of death and decay in the smell too. A skunk hit by a car? No, that was not it either. The odor touched some dim memory hidden in a locked off part of Diana's mind. There was an emotion connected with the smell. While she concentrated on keeping the car on the road, her subconscious recalled the emotion. Terror.

Something was in the road up ahead. A shadow darker than the fog. Diana braked the car even slower and rubbed at the windshield with her hand, trying to see through the gray murk. A pair of taillights? No, there were two patches of glowing red, but they were too close together and too high off the road to be taillights. She let the Pontiac roll toward the shadow at less than ten miles an hour.

Gradually the shadow in the fog took on a shape. It seemed to stand erect like a man. The red sparks could have been eyes. But the figure was not quite human. The shape was wrong.

A gust of wind from somewhere cleared the fog for a moment. For no more than one dreadful second Diana saw what was standing in the road ahead of her. Her foot hit the power brake and the Pontiac jolted to a stop. Matthew, who had dozed off, looked up at his mother in surprise. Other brakes shrieked behind them. In the mirror Diana saw the blurred outline of the pickup bearing down upon them. Then the shattering impact of metal on metal blotted out everything else.

The Pontiac slewed across the road to the left, then tipped in dreamlike slow motion and rolled over the edge of the cliff.

2

The fog was gone when Diana opened her eyes. And there was no trace of the sickening smell. It was still daylight, but just barely. Inside her mouth there was a metallic taste where she had bitten her cheek.

It took a long minute for Diana to orient herself. She was hanging upside down inside the Pontiac, suspended by the seat belt. Beside her Matthew, free of his own belt, knelt on the inverted roof of the car and stroked her hair. Tearfully he called over and over again, "Mom . . . Mom . . . *Mom!*"

Diana pressed the seat-belt release button and dropped to the roof. She worked her legs around until they were beneath her. There were a hundred little aches and bruises, but everything seemed to work as it should.

Matthew touched her face. "Mom, are you hurt bad?"

"I don't think so. What about you, darling?"

"My arm hurts, but it's not too bad."

Diana ran her fingers along the firm young flesh of her son's arm and assured herself there was no break. "It'll be all right," she said.

Awkwardly Diana shifted her position to get at the door handle on the driver's side. The door would not budge. She pushed her shoulder against the panel and thumped it with the heel of her hand, and at last it swung open with a *crump* of twisted metal. She started to crawl out, then drew back when she saw the abrupt dropoff below them. The Pontiac had come to a stop on its back thirty feet below the road, wedged against a stout Douglas fir.

"Be careful, Matt," she said, and eased out of the car, holding on to the scrub chaparral. "You wait here and be very still. I'll climb back up to the road for help."

"I want to go with you!" Matt was trying hard not to cry.

"Do what I tell you!"

Diana heard the edge of hysteria in her own voice and knelt for a moment beside the overturned car. She drew three deep breaths. "Please, honey," she said softly. "I won't be gone more than a few minutes. You be my big boy and wait here for me, okay?"

Matthew swallowed a sob. "Okay. Is the car going to fall any more?"

"No. You be still now."

Diana closed her eyes for a moment, then began crawling slowly and painfully back up to the road.

"You are a very lucky lady."

The voice was male. It came from a pink balloon. The balloon grew features and became a round, pink face as Diana focused her eyes. The face wore thick lenses and rested atop a pudgy little body. A hand reached from the end of a starched white sleeve and touched Diana's forehead. The fingers were firm and cool. They smelled of soap.

"I'm lucky?" The voice was her own this time.

"I'd call it lucky. A foot or two either way and your car would have dropped all the way to the bottom of the canyon. They tell me the tree that caught you was the only one along that stretch of road that was sturdy enough to do it."

"My little boy?"

"Matt's fine. He's outside right now with a stack of comic books. Except for a scratch on his arm, you'd never know he's been in a wreck."

"What is this place?"

"You're in La Canada Memorial Hospital. I'm Dr. Robustelli."

Diana started to sit up in bed. Her left arm felt heavy. She looked down and saw a cast to the elbow that left just the tips of her fingers exposed.

"It's a dislocated thumb," Dr. Robustelli explained. "Not serious. The cast can come off in a week, maybe less."

"When can I go home?"

"This afternoon, as far as I'm concerned. Right now you have a visitor outside from the California Highway Patrol. Do you feel up to talking to him?"

"Sure," Diana said. "Let's get it over with."

A sandy-haired CHP sergeant came into the room. The name *Volney* was stitched on a patch over his badge. He had a Burt Reynolds mustache and bright, alert eyes. He placed a portable cassette recorder on the table next to the bed.

"Do you mind talking into this?"

Diana shook her head.

"I'm sorry to have to bother you now, Mrs. Cross, but the sooner I get the report filed, the sooner it will all be over." He punched on the recorder and smiled at her.

"What do you want me to tell you?" Diana said.

"Everything you can remember about the accident."

"I'm afraid that isn't very much."

"We've been able to reconstruct pretty much what

18

happened from skid marks on the road and the condition of the two vehicles. It's apparent that the second vehicle was traveling at an extreme rate of speed and struck yours from the rear. I just need your version for the report."

"The other car, what happened to it?"

"It was a pickup truck. After colliding with your vehicle, it too went over the cliff. There was no tree to impede its fall, and it bounced all the way to the bottom of the canyon."

"The people inside?"

"We haven't been able to remove the bodies yet, but we have ascertained that the two male occupants were killed."

The two male occupants. Impersonal, like the address on junk mail. A short time before they had been two men called Joker and Bear. They drank beer and laughed. Now they were nobody. Two male occupants, deceased.

"Are you all right, Mrs. Cross?"

"Yes. I was just thinking about the men in the pickup."

"Yes, ma'am."

"All right, the accident. I was driving very slowly because of the fog."

"The fog, ma'am?"

"I got into it right after I started down the mountain. The lower I came, the heavier the fog got. I could only see a few feet in front of the car when I came to the...thing in the road." A shudder raised the fine hairs on Diana's arms as the memory came back.

Sergeant Volney's eyes searched her face. "What sort of a thing, Mrs. Cross?"

"It was...standing upright, but I don't think it was a man."

"A woman?"

"No, I mean I don't think it was human."

She saw Volney's expression change.

"It might have been a bear or something," she said.

"That's possible."

"Its eyes glowed a sort of red. Of course, that could have been the reflection of my headlights. As I said, the fog was very thick and I really didn't get a good look at whatever it was. I stopped to keep from running into it, and that's when the other car, the pickup, hit me from behind."

"You were stopped at the time of the collision?"

"Yes. Or very nearly stopped. I had to or...or hit it."

"What happened then?" Volney prompted.

"After the other car hit me I don't remember anything until I came to some minutes later hanging upside down by the seat belt. I left my little boy in the car and crawled back up to the road for help. I remember a car stopping for me, and then I must have passed out again."

Sergeant Volney was looking at her strangely.

"Is something wrong?" she asked.

"About the fog, Mrs. Cross...are you sure there was fog?"

"Of course I'm sure. I could hardly see the road in front of me. Why?"

"There were no other reports of fog in that vicinity. When our unit responded to the accident call, the weather was clear."

"Ask Matthew. Ask my son about the fog."

"He was asleep at the time of the accident, and doesn't remember anything."

"I can't help that," Diana said, starting to get angry. "It could have been an isolated pocket of fog, couldn't it? It could have lifted before you got there."

"Yes, ma'am, that's possible. Is there any more you

can tell me about this figure you saw standing in the road?"

Diana could read clearly the disbelief behind his neutral policeman's mask. Sergeant Volney did not believe there was any fog, and he did not believe there was anything standing in front of her on the mountain road. To him she was just another lousy woman driver poking down the mountain at a dangerously slow speed. The hell with him.

"I've told you all I can remember," she said. "Now I want to get dressed and get my little boy and go home."

The sergeant snapped off the recorder, stood up, and tucked it under his arm. "Thank you for your cooperation, Mrs. Cross. This should be all we need, but if there is anything else, you're still at the address on your driver's license?"

"Yes."

Volney nodded to her and left the room. Diana reached for the call buzzer. She was anxious to see Matthew and to get out of there.

3

The office of Dr. Alex Letterman, by design, did not look at all like an office. It had a rough stone fireplace, a nubby brown sofa, and a deep leather chair. Between the sofa and the chair was a low table of polished oak. On the table was a heavy ashtray, a book of Dufy prints, and a vase of fresh pink carnations. There was no sign of a desk or filing cabinet or telephone or anything else to indicate the doctor was running a business here.

Diana Cross perched on the sofa while the doctor sat across from her in the leather chair. He had cropped white hair, a glowing Malibu tan, and intelligent blue eyes. Diana lit a cigarette. In the month since the accident she was all the way back up to a pack a day. Letterman leaned forward and moved the ashtray closer to her. He smiled.

"You know, I still don't feel comfortable about seeing a psychiatrist," Diana said.

"It's only your second visit," Letterman said. "Some people never get comfortable with it. Besides, technically I'm a psychoanalyst, not a psychiatrist."

Diana smiled weakly.

"But what I'm called on my certificates is not important. What matters is why you are here."

"As I told you last time, I want to get rid of the

22

dreams I've been having since the accident. But I guess on a deeper level I want to understand what happened to me on that mountain road."

"Let's examine that one first. What do *you* think happened out there?"

"I've already told you the whole story—the accident, what I can remember of it, and what I saw just before it happened. Other people I've told about it think I'm crazy, or hallucinating. Do you think I'm crazy, doctor?"

"Hardly. Why don't you tell me what you're feeling right now, Diana?"

"I feel depressed. And scared, if you want to know. I haven't had one good night's sleep since the accident. I keep dreaming about that thing in the road."

"You said it seemed to remind you of something. Or someone."

"It was just a momentary impression. Since then I've tried, but I can't connect it to anything else in my experience."

"Has anything like it happened to you before?"

"Not exactly like it but...okay, similar."

The doctor sat back and looked attentive. Diana mashed out her cigarette and lit another.

"The first time I can remember something weird happening to me was when I was about Matt's age, not quite six. We were having dinner, my father and mother and I. I happened to look at the doorway just as my grandfather walked in. He just stood there by the table, watching us. This was when we lived in Milwaukee. My grandfather should have been on his farm a hundred miles away, but at the time it didn't seem strange to me. I said, 'Hi, Grandpa.'

"My mother and father looked at me, then at each other. They asked who I was talking to. I told them Grandpa was standing right there with us, and I couldn't understand why they didn't see him. They put

23

me to bed and kept coming in to feel my forehead to see if I had a fever. The next morning we got a phone call from my grandmother. Grandpa had had a heart attack while he was working on the tractor the day before. He died at suppertime."

"How did your parents react then to your ...apparition?" the doctor asked.

"They never mentioned it again. I think they were a little afraid of me after that."

Diana stopped talking and tried to read the bland expression on Letterman's face. "Tell me, doctor, do you believe I saw something out there on the road the day of the accident?"

"I believe *you* believe it."

"That's not the same thing, is it?"

"No, it isn't," he admitted.

"Anyway, I appreciate your honesty."

"Suppose we take another approach. Try to recall your state of mind the day of the accident. Were there any unusual pressures on you? Any strong emotions working?"

"Not really. I was finally getting things together again after my divorce. My social life was okay. My work was going well."

Dr. Letterman glanced down at a three-by-five card. "I see you're an artist."

"I do illustrations for children's books. I like the work, and I'm good at it, but since the accident I've had to turn down assignments. I'm too nervous."

"Any lingering bad feelings about your marriage?"

"No, that's over. It should have ended a lot sooner, but we hung in there for seven years in spite of the fact that we never could really communicate with each other."

"How do you feel about your husband now?"

"Not strongly one way or the other. It was a relief

24

to get away from him and out of his regimented life, but I don't hate him or anything like that."

"How did your little boy take the divorce?"

"As far as I can tell, it hasn't bothered him at all. Jerry and I heard all the horror stories about children of divorce. We read all the books and stayed up nights worrying about how to break it to him, then it turned out Matt was more stable than either of us."

Diana lit another cigarette and blew an impatient stream of smoke toward the ceiling. "This is boring," she said. "I don't see how any of this relates to what I saw in the fog, or to the dreams that are keeping me awake."

"Perhaps it doesn't," said the doctor agreeably. "Is there something else you'd rather talk about?"

Diana thought it over. There *were* things she wanted to tell somebody about. But she remembered the way Dr. Letterman's mouth had quirked at the corners when she told him about seeing her grandfather.

"I think my hour is up." She crushed out what remained of her cigarette and stood up.

"See you on Thursday, then?"

"Doctor, I'm not sure this is doing me any good."

"That's up to you to decide, of course, but why don't you think it over for a couple of days? Then if you still don't feel we're making progress, we'll give it a rest."

"All right. I'll call you."

When she returned to her West Los Angeles condominium Diana recognized Jerry's white Seville parked along the curb out in front. Jerry sat behind the wheel—freshly shaved, crisply correct in his three-piece suit. The perfect picture of a rising young executive. As she pulled into the driveway Diana could see the familiar stiff set of his shoulders that meant he was irritated. She eased into the carport, then got out and waited while Jerry left the Cadillac and walked across the parking area toward her.

"I've been waiting half an hour," he said.

"If you had let me know you were coming, I could have saved you the wait."

"I didn't know I was coming until I heard this morning from my insurance man. Why didn't you tell me you were going to a psychiatrist?"

"Psychoanalyst. And why should I?"

"Because I'm paying for it, for one thing. For another, I have a right to know if you're having mental problems."

Diana looked around at the townhouses that made up her complex. "Let's go inside. There's no need to include the neighbors in this discussion."

Erect and unsmiling, Jerry followed her into the two-level condo where she and Matt had lived since the separation. It was much smaller than the house they had shared in Woodland Hills, but the colors were warmer, the furniture softer. It felt more like home to Diana than the house ever did.

Jerry looked around coolly. "Nice place."

"Thanks. Now what's your objection to my seeing an analyst?"

"I don't object to your seeing him, Diana, I just want to know what the problem is. I mean, if you're going to need some kind of psychiatric care, will you have enough time to spend with Matt?"

"I have just as much time as I ever did. My appointments with Dr. Letterman are in the afternoon when Matt has his school. As you know, I work at home, so I am always available to him. Was that all?"

Jerry shifted his feet uncomfortably on the pale-blue carpet. "I was worried about you. Are you still having problems from the accident?"

Diana's tone softened. "No physical problems. The

26

bruises are all healed, the thumb works fine. I've been having dreams. That's what I've been seeing Dr. Letterman about."

"I suppose you told him about your so-called occult experiences as a girl."

Diana smiled without mirth. She well remembered his frozen look when she tried to tell him of the strange events earlier in her life. She said, "I told him about seeing my grandfather, but not the other things. I don't think he believed me any more than you did."

"Well, you've got to admit that ghosts and things aren't a part of the normal life experience."

"Sure."

"I don't suppose you've got a drink in the place."

"Not unless you want a glass of wine."

Jerry made a face. "No thanks."

The telephone rang. Diana excused herself and picked it up.

"Yes?"

"Hi, Diana, it's me," said the filtered voice of Glenda Yarborough. "Is that Jerry's car out in front?"

"Yes, Glenda, he's here now."

Jerry frowned at the mention of Glenda's name. "Tell her I'm just leaving so she can come over if she wants to."

"He's just leaving, Glenda." Diana turned to give Jerry a little wave as he went out the door.

"Good, I'll be right over."

Diana hung up the telephone and walked to the window in time to see Jerry get into his car and drive off. On the other side of the swimming pool Glenda came out of her own townhouse and hurried toward Diana's.

Glenda Yarborough was a small, energetic woman with darting eyes. She was an editor for a local publisher Diana sometimes did art work for, and she had found this condo for Diana and Matt. She and Jerry had taken an instant dislike to each other, and their relationship had not improved.

"So how did it go with the shrink?" Glenda asked as soon as she was inside.

Diana made a wavering motion with her hand. "Just so-so. I don't think he wants to hear what I want to tell him."

"Look, can I make a suggestion?" Glenda said.

"Could I stop you?"

"A psychiatrist is not what you need."

"He's an analyst. What *do* I need?"

"A psychic."

"Come on."

"No, think about it. What you saw out there in the fog was no human being. You know that. And those other times—the night your grandfather died, the business at the swimming pool, what happened when you fooled with the Ouija board. There's a pattern here, kid, and it's not something a shrink can help you with."

"I don't go for that fortune-telling business."

"Maybe not, but what could it hurt to give it a try? Or maybe you're starting to enjoy the nightmares."

"No way," Diana said. "It's getting to where I hate to go to bed."

"Well then," Glenda said, as though she had proved her point.

"Suppose I was willing to give it a try. What would I do, look in the Yellow Pages under Ghost Catchers?"

Glenda winked at her. "It just so happens I know a man."

"I should have guessed."

"His name is Saul Julian. He's done Tarot readings for me, and he's absolutely marvelous."

"I told you I don't want a fortune-teller."

"Saul is much more than that, believe me. A lot of important people go to him. Got a piece of paper?"

28

"On the table by the telephone."

Glenda scribbled on the top sheet of the note pad, then tore it off and handed it to Diana.

"Here's his phone number. He's in Santa Monica. Just give him a call, mention my name. If you don't like the way he sounds, forget it. You've got nothing to lose but your bad dreams."

Diana looked down at the telephone number Glenda had written. Her eyes ached from lack of sleep.

"I suppose it couldn't hurt to call him," she said.

4

Saul Julian's stucco bungalow in Santa Monica was in the middle of a block of houses much like it. They were well kept, with neat lawns, but all around fifty years old, and beginning to show it. The furniture inside was a mixture of styles from the 1930s to the 1970s.

Julian greeted Diana at the door in a bright-green jump suit. He was a small man with cropped black hair brushed forward and down like a skullcap. His eyes were dark and set deep in their sockets. The somber effect of the eyes was offset by his smile, which was quick and mischievous. Behind him, somewhere in the house, something cooking smelled delicious.

"I'm Diana Cross," she said.

"Hi, Diana," he said with easy familiarity. "Come in and take a seat, I'll be with you in a minute. I've got a pot of chili on the stove, and it's time to add the spices."

"Please, go ahead," she said, but Julian was already on his way back toward the kitchen.

Diana looked around the small, overfurnished living room and chose a comfortable old love seat. She picked up a copy of *People* magazine from the coffee table and leafed idly through the celebrity stories until Julian returned.

"Sorry to rush out," he said, "but I was at a critical point. If I do say so myself, I make the best chili this side of Chasen's, and a lot cheaper."

"It smells wonderful."

"Thanks. It will be done in about fifteen minutes, and we can both have a bowl."

"Oh, I'd like to, but I—I have a dinner appointment."

"That's not true," he said matter-of-factly.

"What did you say?"

"You don't have a dinner date tonight. I'm a psychic, remember? Sees all, knows all."

Diana stared at him for a moment, then answered his smile. "I guess you're not what I expected."

"I know. You were looking for a tall, brooding man in black robes with a piercing gaze and an echo-chamber voice. And maybe an organ playing a Bach cantata in the background."

"That's close," Diana admitted.

"Seriously, I hope you will stay and try a bowl of my chili. It's the one thing I do cook decently."

"Maybe just a taste," Diana said.

"Good." Julian sat down in a chair facing her. When his face grew serious, Diana saw, his eyes really *did* have a piercing gaze. "Now, suppose you tell me why you are here."

Diana began, haltingly, to tell him about her experience on the mountain road and the dreams that had haunted her ever since. She was self-conscious at first, but the way Julian sat perfectly still, giving her his unwavering attention, relaxed her. Soon she found herself talking more freely than she had in a long time.

In twenty minutes she had told him in detail about the thing in the fog and about the childhood experience of seeing her grandfather at the moment of his death. She stopped then and waited for Julian to comment.

"Back in a minute," he said, and walked out of the room.

She waited, puzzled, until he returned carrying two heavy soup cups of chili. He set them down on the coffee table and went back to the kitchen for spoons and a bowl of crackers.

"Don't eat it too fast," he warned. "It's hot."

Diana tasted a small spoonful. "Delicious," she said. "It tastes as good as it smells."

Julian acknowledged the compliment with a nod and grew serious. "There have been other things, haven't there?"

"Other things?"

"Besides the apparition on the mountain road and the ghost of your grandfather, you've had other psychic experiences."

"Yes. How did you know?"

Julian ignored the question. "Tell me about them," he said.

"All my life there have been small things happening that I couldn't explain. I'd be thinking of someone across the country, and at that moment the phone would ring and that person would be on the line. Or I would know before I opened a newspaper that there would be a story in it about someone close to me. And I've always known when my little boy was hurt or in some kind of danger, no matter where I was at the time."

Julian placed the tips of his fingers together and nodded.

"But things like that can have a logical explanation, can't they," Diana said. "They happen to everyone."

"Not to everyone," Julian said. "Please go on."

With an effort Diana pushed aside the mental curtain she had long ago drawn across events she did not want to remember.

"There was the time in high school. I was fourteen, shy, without a lot of friends. I did have one best girlfriend. Her name was Beth Tanner. We were at her place getting ready to go to a pool party at her boyfriend's house. Just as we were starting out the door I looked at Beth's face and almost fainted. The flesh was all bloated and mushy, the eyes fogged over like someone who's drowned and been in the water a long time.

"Suddenly I knew Beth should not go to that party. I told her so. I pleaded with her to stay home, but she just looked at me as if I was crazy. I couldn't put what I had seen into words convincing enough to keep her from going. In the end I went along. I had a miserable time. I kept watching Beth, waiting for something awful to happen."

Diana stopped talking and closed her eyes for a moment on the memory. Julian continued to sit quietly, watching her, saying nothing. After a long moment she continued.

"Nothing out of the ordinary happened for the first hour or so, and I was beginning to think I had been mistaken. Then it was time to eat. Somebody called out that the first batch of hamburgers was ready, and all the kids headed for the charcoal grill. Beth was walking around the edge of the pool from the far side, coming toward me. Her foot slipped and she fell in, cracking her head on the rim. Everyone else was gathered around the charcoal grill, and I was the only one who saw her. I ran to the pool and dived in. Beth was on the bottom, unconscious. I dove down, grabbed Beth by the hair, and fought my way back to the surface. It all happened so fast I didn't have time to call anybody for help.

"When I brought her up the others saw us and came running over. We got Beth out of the water and somebody gave her mouth-to-mouth resuscitation. In about five minutes she came around. All she had was a bump on the side of her head."

"You saved her life," Julian said.

"I guess I did, but you know, we were never close friends after that. Beth seemed to feel that since I foresaw the accident, I was somehow to blame for it."

"That's a fairly common reaction," Julian said. "Tell me, did you ever try to measure the extent of your psychic power?"

Diana looked at him sharply.

"You *do* have the power, you know," he said.

"Yes, I suppose I do," she said. "God knows it's not something I want. It's a curse."

"Not always," Julian said quietly. "But the power has direction and it has limits. That's why I ask if you ever tried to measure yours."

"In a sense, I suppose I did. Once. When I was in college somebody in the dorm came back from Christmas vacation with a Ouija board."

"Balls," said Julian.

Diana looked up in surprise.

"Don't mind me," he said. "Please continue."

"I didn't want to fool around with the thing at all, and usually managed to be somewhere else when the others brought it out. One night, though, when we were all feeling a little light-headed, I let myself be talked into it. We turned the lights in the room way down, and another girl and I sat facing each other with the board resting on our knees. But then, you'd know the procedure, of course."

"I know the procedure," Julian said. He did not smile.

"We both rested our fingertips lightly on the planchette, that little platform with the pointer that's supposed to spell out the words. That's as far as we ever got. The planchette jumped out from under our hands

34

as if it were alive, and sailed across the room. The board itself split down the middle and the two halves flew in opposite directions. It was as though the thing had exploded. We were lucky no one was hurt."

"You were lucky, all right," Julian agreed. "I could tell you Ouija-board stories that would turn your hair white. People treat it like a toy, but it can be more dangerous than a loaded gun. If I had my way the things would be banned."

Diana was silent for a minute. Then she said, "Saul, was it because of me that the board acted the way it did?"

"You know the answer to that."

"Yes. Inside I've always known that I did it. I don't know how, and I don't know why, but whatever was present in the room that night came through me. That is the last time I will ever touch a Ouija board." Diana stopped talking and lit a cigarette.

"There's an aura about you, Diana, I saw it right away. I don't care for the word, the way it's overused today, but there is really no other way to describe the phenomenon. It crackles around you like static electricity. You have strong psychic vibrations, Diana. Very strong. May I see your palm?"

Taken by surprise, Diana held out her hand. Julian took it in his own and scanned the lines of her palm for a minute. He made little humming sounds.

"What do you see?" she asked. "Tall dark stranger? Ocean voyage?"

Julian looked into her eyes. He did not smile. "I see trouble, Diana. Dark trouble."

She searched his face for some sign that he was playing with her. She found none.

Diana stood up, feeling oddly weak in the knees. "Well, I guess that wraps that up."

Julian rose from his chair and stood close to her. "Diana, let me help you."

"What can you do?"

"I'm not sure, but the two of us working together have a better chance of fighting this thing than you do alone."

Diana bit her lip. "I can use some help, that's for sure."

"Can you come back tonight?"

"Back here?"

"Yes. I'm conducting a séance."

"Really, I don't think I—"

"Now hold on," Julian said. "Have you ever attended a séance? A real one?"

"No," she admitted.

"Then don't make prejudgments. I have a man and wife coming here tonight. Their son was killed in a motorcycle accident. They want to try to contact the boy with my help."

"Can you really do that?"

"In this case, I have no idea. I know that I do have certain psychic gifts, and in the past I have been able to make contact. I have a feeling that with you here, the power generated by the two of us will increase the chances for success."

Diana hesitated. "If I come, what should I expect to see? Trumpets blowing? A tambourine rattling?"

Julian smiled. "If you do, it means the spirits have brought their own band. I don't work with that kind of paraphernalia."

"Seriously, what does happen?"

"Sometimes nothing."

"And then the customer gets his money back?"

"No way. I don't give guarantees. Win or lose, my fee is the same."

"How do you know when you win?"

"It might be no more than the sense of a presence in the room. Or there might be a voice. Or the outline of a figure, transparent like the traditional ghost. Or the spirit might appear looking just as solid and alive as you and I."

Diana shook her head. "That's hard to believe, that a dead man, or his ghost or whatever, could walk right into the room looking normal."

Julian's eyes twinkled. "That's right, just as normal as your grandfather."

She gave him a rueful grin. "*Touché*. I'll come to your séance. You're sure the people won't mind?"

"I'll introduce you as an associate. Believe in me, Diana, and I can help you."

Diana picked up her soup cup from the coffee table and finished the last of the chili. "I'll be here, Saul."

"I'm glad. Eight-thirty all right?"

"Fine."

Saul Julian walked her to the door and stood there as she crossed the street and got into the Japanese car she had rented. She looked back at the little psychic with the deep-set eyes and waved.

I hope, she thought, *that I am not making a terrible mistake.*

5

In the evening when she returned to the bungalow in Santa Monica, Diana had strong doubts that she was doing the right thing. The whole idea of a séance was repellent to her. No good had ever come from her brushes with the occult. She remembered vividly the way the Ouija-board planchette had squirmed under her fingers like something alive. She had a strong impulse now to turn the car around and drive home, but the thought of the dreams that awaited her there stopped her.

She parked and locked the car, and walked across the street to Saul Julian's house. The night was cool and a light mist sifted in from the ocean. Julian opened the door to her knock, and she was gratified to see a cheery fire burning in the fireplace. She stepped inside and looked around the warm, lived-in little room.

Julian watched her with a smile. "Looking for trumpets and tambourines?"

"Something like that, I guess. The place just doesn't seem very..."

"Spooky?" Julian suggested.

Diana laughed softly. "That's it, I guess. I've been conditioned by a childhood filled with Vincent Price horror movies."

"I don't blame you, it's what most people expect. As a matter of fact, the room where we'll be working is a good deal more subdued than this one. No fluttering bats or paintings with eyes that move, though. That sort of thing could give ghosts a bad name."

Julian hung Diana's coat in a closet and poured a glass of wine for each of them.

"Mr. and Mrs. Lindley will be here in about half an hour," he said. "I asked you to come earlier to give us a chance to talk."

"That's the couple whose son was killed?"

"Yes. Mrs. Lindley heard about me through a friend. I've talked to them once. They're awfully anxious to contact their boy. Some misunderstanding that wasn't cleared up at the time he died."

"I feel like an intruder," Diana said.

"Not at all. In fact, I expect your presence to be very helpful, considering your affinity for this sort of thing."

"Do you really expect to communicate with their dead son?"

Julian looked at her gravely. "I intend to try very, very hard."

"I'm sorry," Diana said. "I don't mean to sound like a skeptic."

"That's all right," he said. "It goes with the territory. People in my business tend to get oversensitive."

By mutual consent they turned their conversation to trivialities as they finished their wine. Promptly at nine o'clock there was a knock at the door.

Julian admitted a couple in their middle forties. The man had thinning blond hair and the beginning of a paunch. The woman was dark and pretty, with a deep sadness in her eyes.

Julian introduced them as Victor and Helen Lindley. He presented Diana as an associate of his.

"I'm awfully glad to meet you, Diana," Helen Lindley said. "Has Saul told you much about our Brian?"

"Not really," Diana said.

"I don't think it's necessary, Helen," Victor Lindley said. He looked embarrassed.

His wife smiled fondly at him. "Victor didn't really want to come tonight. He only did it to please me."

Lindley touched his wife's arm. His love for her was apparent in the gesture. "Anything I can do to make it easier for you, dear."

Helen Lindley patted his hand. She dug into her purse and brought out a color print encased in plastic of a smiling blond boy in swim trunks.

"Helen," Mr. Lindley chided. Then to Diana, "She pulls out that picture on the slightest excuse."

Diana smiled at him. "I don't blame her. Brian was a nice-looking boy. I'd be proud of him too."

Helen Lindley gazed at the photo. "He was handsome, wasn't he? I miss him so much."

Not knowing what to say, Diana turned to Saul Julian.

"If everyone is ready, we might as well get started," he said.

The Lindleys murmured their assent.

"Come this way, please."

Julian walked to the far end of the room and held a heavy drapery to one side. The Lindleys and Diana passed through and he let the drapery fall behind them. The room was small, with wood-paneled walls and a dark-brown carpet. A chandelier hung over a round table in the center of the room. Four chairs were positioned around the table.

Julian adjusted a rheostat on the wall and the light dimmed. "Please be seated," he said. "Mr. and Mrs. Lindley across from each other, if you please."

The couple took their places self-consciously. Saul Julian sat down facing Diana.

"Now let's all take a deep breath and relax as much as we can. Victor, Helen, concentrate on your son Brian. Think of him as he was during a happy time of your life. Keep that picture in your mind. Diana, I want you to try to join your will with mine. Don't try to think about anything. There is no need for any exhausting effort here. Let's all just be relaxed and easy, and let's think about Brian Lindley. Get comfortable."

They all shifted uneasily in their chairs.

"Now let's place our hands flat on the table," Julian continued. "Let your fingers touch those of the person on either side of you."

"Is the table supposed to move or something?" Victor Lindley asked.

Helen gave him a look, and he shrugged apologetically.

"I wouldn't expect it to," Julian said reasonably, "but if we make contact you can never be sure just what will happen. The purpose of our touching hands is to allow any psychic vibrations to flow through all of us. It's like closing an electrical circuit."

The four people placed their hands flat on the table, fingers spread. Each of them avoided the eyes of the others. Diana felt the strong though hesitant touch of Victor Lindley on her right, and the smooth fingers of Helen on her left.

"Do you want us to close our eyes?" Lindley asked.

"It doesn't matter," Julian said. "Close them if you're more comfortable, or leave them open. The important thing is to concentrate on Brian."

Diana saw that Helen Lindley closed her eyes, as did Saul Julian. Victor Lindley kept his open, staring down at the table in front of him.

There was a minute of silence, then Julian spoke in

a deep, confident voice. "Brian Lindley . . . Brian Lindley . . ." He repeated the name several times. "Your mother is here, Brian. Your father too. They both love you very much. They are concerned about you now. There is a message they want very much to give you. If you can hear me, Brian, and if you are willing to communicate now with your mother and father, make your presence known."

Julian fell silent then, and the minutes ticked by. The only sound in the room was the soft breathing of the people seated around the table. Diana looked around at the others. Saul Julian sat motionless, his eyes closed, his face without expression. Victor Lindley continued to stare down at the table, frowning. Helen Lindley's face worked with her emotions.

Diana returned her attention to Julian. A tiny frown line was etched now between his brows, and a light sheen of perspiration showed on his face. Diana brought her consciousness into a narrow focus, trying to go into the mind of the psychic. Something seemed to change in the room, as though the intensity of the light had been subtly increased. Diana looked up at the chandelier, but could detect no change there.

Still, something was different. The Lindleys felt it too. Victor looked up quickly at Julian, then Diana. Helen's fingers tensed. She squeezed her eyes more tightly shut. Diana shivered as the room temperature dropped. Or was it all her imagination? she wondered.

"Brian Lindley," Julian said. "I can feel that you are near. Your father and mother are very anxious to talk to you. Can you make your presence known?"

Diana stared across the table at Julian. As she watched him, her vision seemed to blur. She blinked several times, but a patch of distortion remained between them, as though she were looking through a flawed pane of glass.

Victor Lindley had raised his head and was now staring across at his wife. His face was tight with concentration. Helen opened her eyes and looked at her husband. They peered at each other nearsightedly, and Diana realized they were both looking at the same foggy patch in the center of the table that she had seen. She returned her attention to the blurry area.

Gradually the patch began to glow with a pale light. It wavered like water. Shadows appeared within it. Almost imperceptibly a face took on definition. It was faded and indistinct, as in a poor photograph, but undeniably a face.

"Brian Lindley." Julian's voice was barely more than a whisper. "Hear me, Brian. Your father and mother are here. We are friends."

The smoky outlines of the face floating just above the table slowly coalesced, the features became more distinct. A young man. Crisp golden hair, sensitive eyes. The expression was not quite readable as the image shifted and wavered like a reflection in troubled water.

"It's Brian." Helen Lindley gasped.

There was a loud crack, as though an electrical spark had arced through the room. The young man's face vanished. Diana gagged as a sudden stench filled her nostrils.

Tears blinded her for a moment. When her vision cleared she saw resting on the table the bestial head of the thing that had stood in the fog on the mountain road. Diana watched in horror as the misshapen head rose. Great humped shoulders, slick with an oily liquid, emerged as though in some obscene act of birth from the solid oak table. Long, powerful arms lifted as the glistening torso grew from the wood. The thing was like a man, yet inhuman in its terrible deformity. One of the wet-slick arms reached toward Diana. She recoiled. The arm described an arc back toward the ghastly head. A beckoning gesture. The face contorted horribly.

Diana screamed. She snatched her hands away from the table, breaking the circle. Victor Lindley, startled, leaped to his feet. His chair toppled backward. Helen Lindley stared open-mouthed at Diana. Only Saul Julian did not move. Droplets of sweat rolled down his face and soaked into the soft collar of his shirt. His brow was creased in intense concentration.

Then, as suddenly as though a switch had been thrown, there was nothing on the table or above it. The stench was gone, the room warmed to normal temperature, and the light returned to the natural dim glow of the chandelier.

Diana dropped her head into her hands. She drew a deep, sobbing breath, struggling for control.

"Diana," Saul Julian said softly. "Diana, are you all right?"

She looked up at him. The deep, dark eyes were comforting.

"I'm sorry," she said. She looked at Mr. and Mrs. Lindley. "I'm terribly sorry."

Victor Lindley righted his chair and sat down again next to her. He took her hand in both of his. "Child, you have nothing to be sorry for. I saw him tonight. I saw my son. God help me, I didn't believe until tonight. And it happened because you were here. I can feel it." He looked across the table at his wife. "Isn't that right, Helen?"

Mrs. Lindley nodded, her eyes on Diana. "Yes, I'm sure it was you. I've felt Brian's presence before, but this time I saw him. He was really here. We have you to thank, dear."

Diana's eyes flicked from one of them to the other. "You saw . . . nothing else?"

44

The Lindleys looked at each other, puzzled. Victor turned to Diana. "No, there was nothing else. But we did see our son. That is all that matters."

"Yes," Helen agreed, "that's all."

Saul Julian stood up then and came around the table to put a hand on Diana's shoulder. "Are you all right?"

She nodded.

Julian turned to the Lindleys. "Excuse us for a moment, please."

Diana let herself be led out through the curtain into the living room and through an arch into a small, neat kitchen. He sat her down in the breakfast nook.

"Wait here for me. I'll be back as soon as I get rid of them." He took a bottle of brandy down from a cupboard and poured some into a glass. He set the glass before Diana. "Sip on this while I'm gone. It'll put the roses back in your cheeks."

When he was gone Diana took a tiny swallow of the brandy. She was no drinker, and the liquor burned on the way down. Once in her stomach, though, it spread a pleasant warmth throughout her body. She took a second, larger swallow, and began to relax.

After five minutes Julian returned.

"They're gone," he said.

"I hope they weren't upset."

"Are you kidding? They were ecstatic. They can't wait to come back and try it again."

"They really didn't...see anything?"

"Just the face of their dead son."

"What about you, Saul, did you see anything else?"

Julian shook his head slowly.

"Oh, God." Diana felt utterly alone.

"But I know something else was there in the room with us," Julian said.

"You do?"

45

"I could feel its presence. Something unspeakably evil. And there was the odor."

"You could smell it?" Diana asked eagerly.

"Faintly. When the image of Brian Lindley disappeared it was there. A rotted, sulfurous smell."

"And Mr. and Mrs. Lindley, could they smell it too?"

"I don't think so. They are attuned only to their son. My senses are more acute. But you, Diana, my God, you have psychic powers far beyond mine, or beyond anything in my experience. The Lindleys were right, it *was* your presence here tonight that called Brian Lindley so clearly into view."

"No." Diana shook her head, denying it.

"Yes," he insisted. "It was you. It might have taken me half a dozen sessions to produce so clear an image, if I could do it at all. With you it came on the first try."

"Then I . . . I must have brought the other thing too."

Julian looked away for a moment, then he faced her again with a helpless shrug. "Yes."

"What *is* it, Saul?"

"I don't know, Diana. I'm sorry."

"It was motioning for me to come to it," she said. "It wants me." Diana shivered at the memory.

"It's true," Julian said, "we don't know what the thing is or why it seems to have chosen you, but we'll find out. We must find out and get rid of it before we can get on with our work."

"Our work?"

"Diana, you are the most gifted natural psychic I have ever met. With training and practice, there is no telling what marvels you can accomplish. Working together, we can move mountains." He smiled. "And, not so incidentally, make a pile of money."

"Money?"

"Sure. Combine your gift with my knowledge of how

to use it, and we have a highly salable commodity." He read the look in her eyes and smiled to take the edge off his words. "Psychics gotta eat too."

"I'm not interested in selling anything to anybody," she said.

"It's not stealing," Julian said defensively. "This is my business. I offer a service, and people pay for it. The better the service, the more they'll pay."

"The whole idea is hateful to me," Diana said.

"I don't think I'm putting this very well."

"No, you're making yourself quite clear. You want to turn me into some kind of a sideshow freak."

"Dammit, that's not it at all. The first thing I want to do is help you. And I can, I'm sure of it, if you're willing to work with me."

"No thanks. Mixing in the occult has brought me nothing but horror and unhappiness. If I do have some sort of . . . gift . . . I have no intention of commercializing on it."

The tension went out of Julian. He gave her a rueful smile. "You're right, of course. You're living with this horror and here I am trying to interest you in a business deal. Look, forget everything I said about making money. But let me help you. As a friend."

Diana reached out and placed her hand over his. "I know you mean well, Saul, and I appreciate what you've tried to do. But all I want is to be out of this nightmare, and I'm afraid working with you would only drive me more deeply into it. Anyway, thanks for caring."

They stood up together. Julian walked her to the front door. Outside the fog was thicker. Diana shuddered.

Julian slipped a card from his wallet and handed it

to her. "If there's ever anything I can do, give me a call."

"I will," she said, taking the card. "Goodbye, Saul."

She walked away from him through the fog to her car.

6

Diana sat on the edge of the sofa in Dr. Letterman's office that was not an office and told him about the séance at Saul Julian's house. Dr. Letterman sat in the comfortable leather chair listening to her. His eyes were half-closed, and he rolled a golf ball across the fingers of one hand. Idly Diana wondered what the Freudian interpretation of his unconscious action might be.

She finished telling the story and waited for a full minute before the analyst said anything. Then abruptly he dropped the golf ball into a jacket pocket and turned the full force of his intense blue gaze on her.

"You sloughed over part of the story, Diana, the part where you describe exactly what it was you saw materialize at this séance."

"I just don't have the words to describe it," Diana said. "I can only tell you it was loathsome beyond imagining."

"And you say it was the same thing you saw on the road just before your accident."

"Yes."

"Did it...say anything? Make any sound?"

"No." Diana shuddered as she recalled the moment. "It...beckoned to me."

Dr. Letterman massaged his lower lip with a forefinger, then changed his direction. "This Saul Julian, what do you know about him?"

"Very little," Diana admitted. "I heard about him from a friend of mine. He seems sincere enough, but who can tell?"

"Mm-hmm," said the doctor in a way that said his suspicions were now confirmed.

"I don't suppose you approve of my going to a psychic," Diana said.

"It's not my job to approve or disapprove, Diana."

"Well, dammit, I wish somebody would. I don't know what's right or wrong any more."

"Anything that makes you feel better, I'd say go ahead and do it," Letterman said. "This séance doesn't seem to have helped much, though."

"It did one thing for me," Diana said. "I'm not having the dreams any more. The bad news is that it brought that damned thing into my waking life."

"Is it possible Julian was using hypnotism?"

"No, I've been hypnotized before, and I know the procedure and the limitations. What I saw that night, I really saw."

"Still, you might have gone there in a highly suggestible state."

"How could Julian have planted a suggestion in my mind without my knowing it?"

"It's possible, but that's not what I'm getting at. Maybe the suggestion came from your own subconscious."

Diana hesitated. The grisly thing she had seen twice now was no invention of her own mind; of that she was sure. However, the alternative explanation—that the thing really existed as she saw it—she was not ready to accept. She said slowly, "Yes, I suppose it's possible it could have come from my subconscious."

Dr. Letterman smiled, as though at a prize pupil. "The mind plays strange tricks."

"And it's those strange tricks that keep you in business," Diana said.

The doctor laughed more heartily than her comment deserved. Then he composed his face and turned the blue gaze on her again. "I'm going to tell you something now that may surprise you. I think our sessions have reached the point of diminishing returns."

Diana felt a pang of irrational fear that she was being abandoned. "What do you mean?"

"Only that I don't think long-term therapy is going to be beneficial to you."

"Just like that? No two weeks' notice or anything?"

"If you insist, I'll see you a few more times," Letterman said. "Or I will refer you to someone else. But in my honest opinion, you'd just be wasting your money."

"Am I supposed to cure myself?"

"That's all psychotherapy does anyway, is encourage you to cure yourself."

"How do I go about it? Just tell myself the thing really isn't there and it will go away?"

Dr. Letterman smiled. "As a matter of fact, that would probably work very well, but I know it's not possible."

"What, then?"

"What I would suggest you do, and the decision of course must be yours, is get out of Los Angeles for a while. The pace of this city is definitely not therapeutic. Change your surroundings. Go someplace where you can relax. Meet new people. Get involved with new activities."

"And that would help me get rid of...my demon?"

Dr. Letterman chuckled. "As they say, it couldn't hurt."

Diana gazed up at the therapeutic still life on the

51

wall over the doctor's head. "I'll think about it," she said.

"Good. Let me know what you decide."

She stood up and took the hand he offered. "Goodbye, doctor."

Diana rode down the twenty floors from the doctor's office in an elevator awash in the music of 1001 Strings. She smiled wryly at her reflection in the mirror set into one of the padded walls. When your analyst tells you to get out of town, that must be the ultimate rejection.

That evening Diana sat on her couch with a map of California spread out on the coffee table before her. Matt was in his favorite television-viewing position, prone on the shag carpet with his elbows propped and his chin in his hands. Diana could never understand why he didn't get a stiff neck. He watched gravely, not joining in the canned laughter that accompanied the antics of *Mork and Mindy*.

Diana traced with her finger an arc approximately sixty miles from the center of Los Angeles. To the north and west, beyond the San Fernando Valley, lay Oxnard, Ventura, and Santa Barbara. Nice towns, she supposed, but there was no special thing about them that made her want to go there. Off to the northeast were Newhall, Palmdale, and Lancaster. Unfairly, perhaps, they made her think of dusty beer bars and country-and-western music. Her finger moved on. Victorville, Barstow. No, forget the desert in the summertime. The same for Palm Springs, and never mind all its swimming pools. She followed the coastline south of Los Angeles. Newport Beach, Laguna, San Clemente. Halfway between San Clemente and Oceanside her finger stopped.

Tranquilo Beach. What a lovely sound it had. Just what the doctor ordered. Diana searched her memory for what she knew about Tranquilo Beach. Located on the old Coast Highway, it was bypassed by most travelers, since Interstate 5 was completed five miles to the east. The town had no industry worth mentioning. Most of the working residents commuted to either Los Angeles or San Diego. Tranquilo Beach had a modest reputation as an artist colony. Once a year, over the Labor Day weekend, they held a festival that attracted a fair number of tourists. Perhaps, Diana thought, the atmosphere would inspire her to work again. She had not painted anything that pleased her since the accident.

She looked over at Matthew. He had lost interest in the television show and was leafing through a Spiderman comic book.

"Matt, come here a minute."

Carrying the comic book with a finger marking his place, Matt came over and peered down at the map where his mother was pointing.

"How would you like to spend the summer down here?" she asked.

"What is it?"

"It's a town called Tranquilo Beach."

"I like it okay here."

"We'll come back here in the fall, in time for you to start school."

Matthew frowned down at the dot on the map. "Is it a real beach?"

"I'm sure they have one."

"Can I have a surfboard?"

"We'll see."

"That means no."

"We'll see," Diana repeated firmly.

"Is it close to Disneyland?" Matt asked, considering a trade-off.

"Not exactly, but we can go to Disneyland this weekend if you want to.

"Can we? Oh boy! I want to go on Space Mountain this time."

"We'll have to discuss that," Diana said. "In the meantime, what do you say to Tranquilo Beach?"

"Sure, that's okay."

Diana hugged the boy and ruffled his pale hair. "I love you a lot, do you know that?"

"Aw, Mom." He squirmed restlessly, held by her arm.

Diana let him go and gave him an affectionate swat on the bottom. "Go on back to Spiderman."

"Did you mean it about going to Disneyland?"

"I meant it."

"Oh boy!"

Diana watched her son drop back to the carpet and pick up his reading of the comic book where he had left off. When her eyes filled with tears she turned away.

7

Diana kept busy through the month of May getting ready for the move to Tranquilo Beach. The dreams did not return, and only in rare idle moments did she think about the thing she could not name.

She found a three-bedroom cottage a block from the ocean that would be available for the summer while the owners were in Hawaii. Jerry was not enthusiastic about letting her and Matt go, but when he saw Diana was determined he made no strong objection.

Her arrival with Matt on an early June afternoon could not have been more promising. The sky was a brilliant blue all the way to the horizon, a sight not seen in Los Angeles for many years. The cottage, set in a clump of cypress trees, had a fresh coat of sunshine-yellow paint to go with the red roof. When they parked out in front some of the local people waved as they strolled by in swim suits on their way to the beach.

All of Matt's misgivings vanished as he bounced out of the car. "Can we go to the beach now, Mom?"

"Let's get moved in first, shall we?" Diana said.

They unloaded the bags from the Olds Cutlass Diana had bought to replace the Pontiac. She had been strict in seeing that they brought with them as few things as possible. Casual clothes only, her paints and brushes, a very few of Matt's favorite toys. Everything else— furniture, linens, dishes—had been left in the cottage for them by the owners.

The rooms were small and scrupulously clean. There was a cozy living room with wood-burning fireplace, a family room, a compact kitchen, and the three bedrooms. Diana moved her personal things into the front bedroom and her painting equipment into the smallest, which had good light and would serve as a studio.

Matt bounced up and down on the bed in his room, approved its springiness, and renewed his clamor to go to the beach.

"All right," Diana said. "Get your swim suit on and we'll walk down, but we have other things to do, so don't expect to stay all day."

She put on a pair of shorts and a terry beach jacket while Matt got into his trunks. They walked the short downhill block to the beach, a quarter-mile strip of pale-yellow sand. The people already there were mostly women. The wives, Diana guessed, of commuting husbands. There were a few teenagers in a flagged-off portion of the beach, riding surfboards, playing radios, and comparing tans, but they were reasonably quiet and well behaved.

Holding tightly to Matt's hand, Diana waded a short distance out into the surf. The gentle incoming waves splashed around her shins.

"Come on, Mom, let's go out farther," Matthew urged.

"Not me, mister. This water is like ice."

"Awww, Mom..."

"You can splash around here for a while if you want to. I'll be right up there on the sand. And when I wave for you to come in, that means come in, and no nonsense."

A bronzed young man in the brief red swim trunks

of the county lifeguards strolled over from his tower perch to join them.

"Hi, I'm Guy Urich," he said. "You must be the people who moved into the Thompsons' house."

"That's right. I'm Diana Cross. My champ swimmer there is Matt."

"Anytime you want to send Matt down to the beach I'll keep an eye on him for you," Guy said. "The bottom slopes away gently along this stretch. It's really very safe."

"Thank you, Guy," Diana said. "I appreciate that."

"It's my job," he said, showing healthy white teeth. "For one more summer, anyway. Then I'll be going to college."

"Congratulations."

"In case you need somebody to sit with Matt sometime, my little sister is good at it, and she's always eager to earn spending money. Her name's Nancy."

"I'll remember that."

"See you." He tossed a casual salute to the boy watching him from the surf. "So long, Matt."

"So long," Matt said. He walked up and stood next to his mother and watched the well-muscled young man stroll on down the beach, greeting the other people. He looked up at his mother. "Can I be a lifeguard when I get big enough?"

"Maybe, if you can swim well enough."

"I can swim good now."

"We'll talk about it later. Right now I think we'd better go out and do some shopping."

"I can stay here," Matt suggested. "Guy said he'd watch me."

"Not this time. Come on, let's go."

With great reluctance Matt allowed himself to be taken by the hand and led back up to the cottage.

They drove to a supermarket up on the highway, and

57

Diana loaded the back seat of the car with groceries. On the return trip she saw a painted sign in front of a small shop reading: *Harriet's Art Supplies*. She pulled over to the curb and stopped.

"Wait here," she told Matthew. "I'll just be gone a minute."

On the sidewalk out in front of the shop a plump, baby-faced woman wearing a paint-stained smock was doing a water-color street scene. The perspective, Diana noted, was all out of whack. The woman did not look up as Diana went past her into the art supply store.

Inside, the merchandise seemed to be in a hopeless jumble. Still, Diana could see that there was a good selection of paints, brushes, boards, easels, and all the other paraphernalia of the artist.

Diana looked around for a clerk, saw no one.

"Hello?" she called. "Anybody here?" Still there was no response.

She found a bell behind a stack of sketchbooks on the counter and tapped the button with a forefinger. It gave out a melodious *ding*.

The plump woman in the smock came in from the sidewalk. She still held a brush in her hand. "Oh, hi, I didn't see you come in. Sometimes I get so wrapped up in my painting I don't know what's going on around me."

"I saw your picture," Diana said. "Interesting."

"That's nice and noncommittal, but the thing's lousy and I know it. I can't seem to get the hang of doing straight lines and angles. It's hell trying to do buildings if you can't make angles. The only reason I paint street scenes is because everybody else in town paints seascapes. I mean, how many pictures of waves breaking on the rocks can a person look at before he gets a headache?"

"Practice makes perfect," Diana said, smiling.

58

"Not in my case, I'm afraid. My buildings will always look like mounds of Jell-O. Are you an artist?"

"I'm an illustrator. I do children's books mostly."

"No kidding?" The plump woman laid the brush down carefully and wiped her hands on her smock. "I'm Harriet Nagle. It's a pleasure to meet a real professional. I mean, everybody in T-Beach claims to be an artist of one kind or another, but the only real professional we had living here is that guy who used to do those sour editorial cartoons for the Los Angeles *Times*. Since he died of cirrhosis of the liver, we haven't had anybody. Are you here to stay?"

"Just for the summer. I'm Diana Cross. My little boy and I will be here until after Labor Day. We're staying in the Thompsons' cottage, if you know where that is."

"Sure, it's that cute little place with the red roof. Everybody in this town knows every house. Part of the charm, if you find that sort of thing charming. Anyway, I'm glad to have you with us, Diana, even for a short time. No husband?"

The unexpected personal question took Diana by surprise. Still, she could not help liking this talkative woman, and she could think of no good reason not to answer.

"I'm divorced."

"Widowed myself," Harriet said.

"I'm sorry."

"Don't be. Ray's been dead five years now, and I'll be honest with you, those years have been a lot happier than the seven we spent together. He left me enough for the store. I just open it when I feel like it and close up if I have something else to do."

"Sounds like a pretty good life," Diana said.

"It's all right. Still I sometimes wish I could have been a divorcée. That sounds sexy and playful. 'Widow' sounds cold and grim."

"It's all in the way you say it," Diana suggested.

"Maybe. Anyway, here I am gabbling away when you probably came in to buy something. What can I do for you?"

Diana gave her the short list of supplies she needed to get back to work. Harriet found the items in all the confusion with no trouble at all and put them in a bag.

The two women walked back out to the street together. "Listen, do you know anybody in town yet?" Harriet asked.

"Just you. And the lifeguard on the stretch of beach below the cottage."

"Guy Urich," Harriet said. "Nice kid."

"He seemed to be. Said he has a sister who does some baby-sitting."

"That would be Nancy. She's good with kids, and you can trust her."

"That's good to know."

"Anyway," Harriet continued, "I know you're going to be busy, but you can't work all the time, and we've got a bunch of girls—listen to me, most of us will never see thirty-five again—who get together for this or that project, or just to raise a little hell. Would you like to come along with me and meet them?"

"It might be fun," Diana said, thinking how long it seemed since she had done anything simply for fun.

"Terrific." Harriet seemed honestly delighted. "We're getting together Wednesday at Edith Werhaus's place for a wine-tasting party. You know—eat cheese and crackers and sip a bunch of different wines and make clever-sounding comments about them while we're getting a little tiddly."

"What time?" Diana asked.

"In the afternoon. Of course, if it interferes with your work..."

60

"It won't," Diana told her. "I only work in the morning."

"Great. I'll pick you up about two o'clock."

"Hey, Mom!"

Diana looked around in surprise at the sound of her son's voice coming from the wrong direction. Matt was walking toward her along the sidewalk. Keeping pace with him was a very tall man with a lean, humorous face and a Lincolnesque shock of black hair. Matt was talking to the man and pointing at Diana.

"That's her," she heard him tell his companion.

When they reached her and Harriet, Diana gave Matt a quick frown, then looked up at the man. His eyes were warm and dark, with laugh crinkles.

"Mrs. Cross?" he said.

Diana nodded. Her eyes flicked between the tall man and her son.

"I'm Kirby Franklin. Matt here got a little mixed up about his directions, and I told him I'd help him look for you."

"Why didn't you wait in the car the way I told you?" Diana demanded of the boy. Without waiting to hear an answer she looked up at Kirby Franklin. "Thank you. He doesn't often wander off like that."

"I just went up to the Thrifty to look at the toys," Matt said. "You were gone so *long*."

"I was not. Anyway, that isn't the point."

"There isn't much trouble he can get into in T-Beach," Franklin said.

"All the same, when I tell him to wait somewhere for me, that's where I expect to find him."

Franklin looked gravely down at the boy. "She's right, you know."

"Aww." Matt stared at his tennis shoes.

"How are you, Harriet?" Franklin said, acknowledging the other woman.

"I'm just fine." She beamed at Kirby Franklin and at Diana. "Diana will be living here for the summer."

"Only the summer?" There was a genuine note of disappointment in Franklin's voice.

"I have a place of my own back in Los Angeles," Diana explained. "Matt and I are just leasing here." *Matt and I*. Did she put it that way, Diana wondered, specifically to tell Kirby Franklin there was no husband in the picture?

"Maybe by the end of the summer you'll like us well enough to stay," he said.

Diana approved of the way he smiled. She smiled back. "That's a possibility."

Franklin said his goodbyes and strode back up the street in the direction from which he had come.

"Nice-looking man, isn't he?" Harriet said.

"In a way," Diana admitted.

"He's a newspaperman. He edits the Tranquilo Beach *Tide*. That's our little weekly."

Diana nodded politely.

"He's available too," Harriet added, coming down meaningfully on the word. "Divorced."

"Oh?"

"He's been here five years, but hasn't been seriously involved with anybody. He likes you, though, I could tell."

"Oh, I think it's a little premature to..."

"No, I recognize the signs," Harriet insisted. "You'll be hearing from him."

Diana laughed in spite of herself. "I'll see you Wednesday," she said, and bundled Matt into the car.

"Are you going to go out with him?" Matt asked as they pulled away from the curb.

"With who?" Diana asked unnecessarily.

"The tall guy."

"What kind of a question is that? I just met the man."

"But the other lady said—"

"Never mind what she said. I have no plans for seeing Kirby Franklin again."

"I bet you will."

"Hush now."

The next evening Kirby Franklin appeared at the door of Diana's cottage. He carried a potted plant in one arm and a Styrofoam bellyboard in the other.

"I'd have called first," he said, "but I guess you don't have the phone hooked up yet. If you're busy, I can come back another time."

"I'm not busy," Diana said, surprised at how pleased she was to see him. "Please come in."

"I don't know much about plants, but I'm told this doesn't need a lot of care."

"It's a philodendron," Diana said. "And it's lovely. I do enjoy plants and I haven't had a chance to put any in here yet. Thank you."

Franklin handed the bellyboard over to a wide-eyed Matt. "You were saying you wanted to learn to ride a surfboard. I think this will get you started."

"Wow." said Matt. "Thanks. Can I go down and try it out now, Mom?"

"It's too late. Tomorrow will be soon enough." She smiled at Kirby. "That was thoughtful."

"I had another reason for coming tonight," he said. "I'd like to do a piece on you for the *Tide*. I've been down at the library looking over some of your work. I like it. Art that appeals to both children and adults can't be easy to do."

"I just draw pictures," Diana said, pleased by the compliment.

"Is it okay if I watch TV?" Matt said.

63

"Sure, go ahead," Diana told him.

Matt started off toward the family room clutching the bellyboard under his arm. Rounding the corner he turned back to Diana. "I told you he'd be back."

8

On Wednesday, Harriet Nagle showed up at Diana's cottage at half past two in her battered Volkswagen. Matt was at the beach with a bunch of new friends under the watchful eye of Guy Urich. Feeling lighter and happier than she had for a long time, Diana got into the little car.

Harriet, talking nonstop all the way, drove to the home of Edith Werhaus. It was a big stone house on a cliff south of the beach that had been there longer than the town. It had a cold, austere look that dampened somewhat Diana's light spirits as they approached along the cliff road.

Harriet parked the car in front of the house. A flight of stone steps led up to the front door. At the top of these Edith Werhaus awaited them.

Edith was a tall, dramatic redhead dressed in a wildly colored lounging suit with flowing sleeves. As the two women climbed the steps toward her she spread her arms wide in a theatrical gesture.

"Welcome, welcome, welcome, Diana Cross. Your reputation has preceded you, courtesy of our dear friend Harriet here."

Diana smiled uncertainly, a little taken aback by the woman's flamboyant manner.

"Now, let's have a look at you," Edith said when they reached the top of the steps. "Very pretty. Yes, an exceedingly pretty woman." She caught Diana's fleeting expression and laughed, not unkindly. "In case you're wondering if you've fallen into a nest of lesbians, forget it. We are all excessively fond of men. It just happens that for one reason or another we find ourselves frequently manless, so we indulge in our harmless pursuits."

"It sounds like fun," Diana said. "I could use some fun in my life."

"With a touch of brains and a dash of imagination you will be a welcome addition," Edith said.

She swept through the open door and into the house. Diana glanced at Harriet, who smiled reassuringly.

"Edith overacts sometimes," Harriet said, "but she's really a good kid. Don't let her overwhelm you."

"I'll try," Diana said. They followed the tall woman inside.

The interior of the house was a pleasant surprise after the forbidding appearance it presented from the road. It was decorated cheerfully in excellent taste, with beige and blue predominating.

The three other women who made up the group were waiting for them in the living room. Their appearance placed them in the upper-middle socioeconomic class. Their ages were in the thirties and forties. Edith ceremoniously introduced Diana to each of them.

There was Lisa Becker, who wore short curly black hair and modish tinted glasses through which her eyes looked large and guileless. She smiled as she talked and clasped Diana's hand sincerely when they were introduced. Lisa's husband was a pediatrician who had a practice and a mistress in Oceanside.

Phyllis Crane had a twenty-inch waist and a thirty-eight-inch bust. She wore wide, tight belts and clinging

66

tops to emphasize both. She wore her hair long with little-girlish ribbons, and spoke in a high, breathless voice. Her husband was an oceanographer who rushed home from his frequent forced absences to perform incredible sexual feats, which Phyllis described to her friends in loving detail.

Zoe Maples was the other divorcée of the group. She had a caustic wit that was turned most often on herself. Diana recognized this as a defense mechanism for a very vulnerable woman.

Although each of the women had very definite opinions of her own, Edith Werhaus was the acknowledged leader. It was she who organized the outings and came up with new ideas to keep the group from growing stale. Edith read everything that was current, and prided herself on being "into" things before they became trendy. Her husband, Philip, was a placid, unremarkable man who owned a small computer firm in Los Angeles, and had done well in quiet real estate speculation.

The women welcomed Diana cordially into their group, and she enjoyed herself thoroughly, finding something in common to talk about with each of them. The wine-tasting session Edith had set up was a rousing success. By the end of the afternoon they had, as Harriet predicted, got a little tiddly.

To Diana's further relief, Matthew adjusted quickly to the new town. He quickly made friends among the neighbors and with the other children at the beach. Guy Urich was as good as his word in looking out for the youngsters, and his sister, Nancy, proved to be a reliable sitter for the times when Diana went out in the evening.

Her evenings became quite as full as the mornings and afternoons as Kirby Franklin became a regular caller at the cottage. Sometimes they would take Matt with them to a movie or for a Sunday at the San Diego zoo. Diana was pleased at the easy way the man and the boy got along together. There were none of the forced pleasantries and unspoken rivalry that existed so often when a man dates a woman who is also a mother.

But they had their evenings alone too. Kirby enjoyed good food, and he took Diana to all of the best restaurants he had discovered along that stretch of the coast. They went to the little theaters that were active in San Clemente, and danced at the Oceanside Holiday Inn, where almost half of the songs played by the band were slow ones.

Coming home from these evenings, they would sit on the couch in her living room after Matt had gone to bed, and hold each other close—kissing, touching, and letting their bodies get acquainted. Through the month of June it went no further than that. Kirby had made the obligatory suggestion that they go to bed after their second date, and Diana was grateful that he had not pushed it when she told him she was not yet ready for that. Certainly, there was no lack of physical desire on her part. Kirby's touch set her skin tingling, and even his voice on the phone could excite her. The fact that he wanted her was apparent, especially when they danced close together. Neither of them doubted that sooner or later they were going to bed. By the end of June, Diana had decided that it would be soon. Very soon.

To make everything even better, she was working well again, for the first time in months. She had taken an assignment from her Los Angeles publisher to do twelve illustrations and a cover for the first book of a planned series of whimsical stories for six-year-olds. If the series caught on it would mean a good regular income Diana could count on.

Diana's new circle of friends had followed the wine tasting with a variety of activities. One day they drove up to Hollywood Park for a day at the races. Diana, although she knew nothing about horses, won $140 playing her hunches. The others lost, but not very much. They had visited an art exhibit in La Jolla, held a raffle to raise money for the Tranquilo Beach Library, and helped the local Humane Society place its entire stock of cats and dogs in good homes. They had heard a lecture on cosmetic surgery, watched a demonstration of psychodrama therapy, and brought in two poets from Laguna Beach to read their verse. With the exception of the poets, who were both too high on sinsemilla to make sense, Edith had come up with a string of winners.

As the Fourth of July weekend approached, Edith turned secretive and smug. She had spent three days in San Juan Capistrano going through a cache of old books that had been discovered in the burned-out ruins of a hillside house. The house was over two hundred years old, built, it was said, by a Franciscan friar who was banished from the Church for some unspecified blasphemy. The most recent owner was a Beverly Hills broker, who willed the contents, principally the old books, to the South Coast Historical Society. President of the society was Edith Werhaus.

When she returned to Tranquilo Beach, Edith acted like a woman who had acquired a secret lover.

"Come on, Edith," Harriet coaxed. "You found something good up there. What was it?"

"I'll bet it's something dirty," Zoe Maples said.

"Oh, Zoe." Phyllis giggled. "You're just wishful thinking."

"Whatever it is," Lisa said, "I'll bet it's something for our group, isn't it, Edith?"

"All of you are right in a way," Edith said mysteriously. "Tomrrow we'll have lunch at El Poche, and I'll tell you all about it."

Diana alone was not eager to hear what Edith had found in the old burned-out house. Her sixth sense, dormant since she'd come to Tranquilo Beach, now warned her of trouble ahead connected with Edith's find in Capistrano. Diana tried to diplomatically excuse herself from the luncheon, but the others would not hear of it.

Edith smugly maintained the suspense at lunch until they had finished their food and were drinking the bitter Mexican coffee. When she had everyone's attention, she cleared her throat and spoke.

"As you know, it was the books that were my main interest in the house in Capistrano. Most of them were decayed by time or destroyed in the fire, but there was one trunk that was untouched by the flames. Inside there was just one book. It was bound in some kind of pale leather and inscribed with curious figures. It was in such good condition I could hardly believe it. I know a bit about old books, and this one certainly predates any I have seen.

"The text was in ancient Latin, so for once my classical education came in handy." She smiled around at the others. "It's not the kind of a book that the T-Beach Library would want to display, but it's perfect for our little group."

"Well, what *is* it, Edith?" Phyllis coaxed.

"Yes, tell us," said Lisa.

"I hope it's not poetry," Zoe said. "I've had it with poetry after those two spaced-out freakos."

"No, it's not poetry," Edith said. She was enjoying herself immensely.

"Well, for heaven's sake, Edith, tell us what you've got for us," Harriet said.

"A rather inappropriate choice of words," Edith said.

70

"You see, the title is..." She paused for dramatic effect. *"Book of the Damned."*

Diana felt the brush of icy fingers at her neck. Harriet looked at her curiously, but no one else seemed to notice her reaction.

"What are we going to do with a thing like that?" Phyllis asked.

"What we are going to do," Edith told them, "is get together at my place this Saturday night and raise a demon."

9

"It's a mistake," Diana said. "We shouldn't be doing this."

It was her turn to drive this Saturday night, and on the short trip from her cottage to Harriet Nagle's bungalow her doubts had grown steadily.

"Ah, it's just for kicks," Harriet said, easing into the front seat of the Cutlass. "Don't take it so seriously." She slammed the door behind her. "You know Edith well enough by now to know that she comes up with some weird ideas. It usually turns out to be kicks, though."

"This time she might be getting us all in over our heads."

"You're turning into a worrywart." Harriet shifted sideways in the seat to look at her. "Unless you know something more about this business than you're telling us."

Briefly Diana considered telling Harriet and the others about her encounters with things occult in the past, and about the pain they had caused her. Over the past month she had grown fond of these women, and especially plump, friendly Harriet Nagle. Still, Diana had never talked about the darker portions of her life. She had never told them the reason she had moved here.

That was something she hoped she could leave behind forever. Here in Tranquilo Beach her life was fresh and new, and she did not want to spoil it by dragging in bad memories.

She said, "The idea just makes me uncomfortable, that's all."

"Well, quit worrying about it," Harriet advised. "You know none of the girls would go along with anything that's not kosher."

"I suppose so," Diana said.

"Then let's go. Edith said it was important that we all get there on time."

Diana put the car in gear and drove north through the quiet streets of Tranquilo Beach and out the cliff road. She tried, while Harriet chattered happily, to swallow the fear that rose like bile in her throat.

They arrived in minutes at the big house. Diana parked the car and they climbed the dark stairs to the front door. Edith, wearing a dramatic flowing gown, swept open the door before Diana could ring the bell.

"Come in, come in, the others are already here."

As Edith held the door for them the sleeve of her gown slipped back to reveal a fresh bandage on the inside of her forearm.

"Did you hurt yourself?" Harriet asked.

Edith waved the question away. "It's nothing. I burned it on the iron."

Diana reflected that Edith Werhaus had never seemed to be the kind of a woman who did her own ironing.

Harriet greeted the other three women, who were standing rather uncomfortably in the living room.

"All right, I want to know how you married people managed to get out of the house on a Saturday night. I never could."

Lisa Becker gave them her sweet smile. "There's no problem with Sam and me. If a night out with the girls will make me happy, he says go ahead."

"That's like giving you a license to fool around," Zoe remarked.

"Oh, I would never—" Lisa began. Then she saw that Zoe was kidding her, and smiled.

"The way I did it was to keep Norman busy in bed all day," Phyllis said, giggling. "By tonight he was so tired, I think he was glad for the time to recover."

Diana turned to Edith. "What about Philip? How did you get him out of the house?"

"Or maybe you've got him locked in the attic," Zoe suggested.

"Philip had some kind of contract negotiation in Los Angeles today," Edith said. "He expects the bargaining to go on late into the night, so he's taking a hotel room there. And Timmy is asleep upstairs in his room, so we'll have the place to ourselves."

Lisa looked around at the bright, comfortable living room. "Where are we going to...do it?" she asked. "In here?"

"No, this isn't the right atmosphere," Edith said. "I have the rec room downstairs all ready for us."

"Is there anything to eat?" Harriet asked. "I was tied up at the shop until late this afternoon, and didn't have time for dinner."

"I have some sandwiches for afterward," Edith said, "but now I think we should get started."

Through a door in the kitchen, Edith led them down a narrow flight of wooden stairs to the basement, a rarity in California houses. Diana watched the tall, red-haired woman, and wondered at the change in her from the other times they had been together.

Edith had always liked to dramatize their little adventures, but tonight there was a feverish intensity in

74

her speech and her movements that Diana had not seen before. There was a flush over her high cheekbones and a glitter to her eyes that made her look exceptionally beautiful. And to Diana, very disturbing.

In the wood-paneled recreation room all the usual furniture had been pushed back against the walls. On the composition floor a large geometric pentagram had been painted in red and black. There were five straight-back chairs, one on each point of the star, and a lectern in the center of the figure. On the lectern rested a heavy book bound in pale leather. Diana shivered.

Around the outside of the pentagram Edith had placed candles in brass holders on the floor. They were tall, misshapen columns of black wax that looked hand-made. She walked around now with a long fireplace match and touched the flame to each of them. The wicks sputtered and caught, each trailing a streamer of greasy smoke to the ceiling.

The other women looked at each other uneasily. The smiles they exchanged were not convincing.

"It's so spooky." Phyllis said in her little-girl voice.

"Leave it to Edith to come up with all the right props," said Harriet.

"It certainly is...atmospheric," said Lisa, looking to the others for concurrence.

Diana felt a spot of cold within her that was growing larger. In a low voice she said, "I don't think we ought to do this."

Before anyone could respond, Edith lit the last candle, turned out the overhead light, and walked up to claim their attention.

"Very well," she said, "it is time to begin. Each of you will take a chair."

Phyllis started to giggle, then cut it off when she looked around and saw no one else was smiling. After some self-conscious hesitation, the five women took their places at the points of the pentagram. Edith went to the center and stood at the lectern. She turned slowly and let her eyes rest for a moment on each of the others.

"Before we truly begin," she said, "I want to offer each of you this opportunity to change your mind. What we are attempting to do here tonight can have a profound effect on our lives. What that effect might be, I cannot predict, but the ritual requires that each of us participate of our own free will."

The women shifted uneasily in their chairs, but no one spoke. Diana stared down at the floor. For the first time she saw that within the geometric figures formed by the lines of the pentagram were dozens of intricate runic symbols drawn with a felt-tip pen. They seemed to squirm and jitter under her gaze. It took an effort for Diana to pull her eyes away.

When she looked up she found Edith watching her. There was the suggestion of a challenge in the bright-green eyes.

Now, thought Diana. Now is the time to stand up and cry *Stop!* before this business goes any further. She looked around at the faces of the others, her friends. They were all looking at her, as though they were waiting for some signal.

She had known these women scarcely thirty days, yet they had become as close to Diana as any women friends in the past. Good-natured Lisa, Phyllis the sexy little girl, witty Zoe, and fat, talkative Harriet. Diana did not want to lose these new friends. She did not want to disrupt the good new life she had found in Tranquilo Beach. Somehow she knew she would lose it all if she now defied the tall red-haired Edith. She looked down again at the writhing symbols so carefully traced on the floor. Edith must have spent hours preparing for this evening. Let her have it then. *And God help us all,* a voice within Diana said.

"Are there no second thoughts, then?" Edith spoke to the group, but she continued to look at Diana.

Diana looked up and gave the tall woman a faint smile. She moved her head fractionally from side to side.

"Very well, we begin."

"Mommy."

Edith whirled at the sound of the childish voice. The others started as though a gun had gone off in the room. Little Timmy Werhaus, his eyes blinking away the sleep, stood at the foot of the stairs that led down into the basement.

"What are you doing down here?" Edith demanded. "You're supposed to be in bed."

"I couldn't sleep," the little boy said. "I heard talking."

"That was me and my friends. Now you march back up to bed, young man."

"Why do you have the candles on? What's that stuff on the floor?"

Edith took a step toward her son. "Timmy, I want you back in that bed right now, and don't make me tell you again. If there's one more peep out of you, I'm going to get out the strap."

Timmy's lower lip quivered for a moment, but he turned obediently and started up the stairs.

"And close the door after you," Edith called.

When the door slammed lightly at the top of the stairs she resumed her place behind the lectern and looked around at the others.

"Let us continue," she said. The planes of her face were flat and hard in the candle light. Her thin little smile was without mirth.

Edith placed her hands reverently on the old book.

She looked one more time at each of the women, then opened the book to a place marked with a crimson ribbon. "From the *Book of the Damned*..."

Edith began to read a long passage in a deep, sonorous voice. The words were in Latin, a language none of the other women understood. Although it had no meaning for her, Diana's sense of dread increased as the tall woman spoke. The candles threw grotesque dancing shadows on the walls. The room seemed to have grown uncommonly cool for July.

With a start, Diana realized that Edith had stopped talking more than a minute ago, and she had continued to sit listening. She glanced around and saw the same look of sudden confusion on the faces of the other women as their awareness returned.

When Edith saw she had their full attention, she put her hand down to the shelf of the lectern and brought out a glass vial. She held it up so they could all see. It contained perhaps four ounces of a deep scarlet liquid. There was a gasp from the women.

"What is it?" Harriet asked.

"What does it look like?" was Edith's response.

"It looks like blood," said Lisa.

Edith just smiled.

"Oh, how awful," Phyllis said. "I think I'm going to be sick."

"Don't be foolish," Zoe told her. "Lots of things look like blood. Tomato juice, for one. What is it really, Edith?"

"It is whatever you believe it is." Edith was now fully into her role as the black priestess.

Diana's eyes traveled from the vial of red liquid to the white bandage on Edith's arm. She wished desperately that this evening were over and behind them.

"We shall continue," Edith said.

She stepped in front of the lectern then and twisted the stopper out of the vial. Standing upright, she carefully let the liquid trickle out to form a serpentine track on the floor at the center of the pentagram. She spoke a string of unintelligible words that sounded like no language any of them had ever heard.

When the vial was empty, Edith walked around and pinched out the candle flames one by one. Each made a little hiss as it died. When only one candle remained lighted, she carried it to the lectern and set it carefully before the book.

When she spoke again it was in English. Her voice seemed to echo off the walls of the room.

"In the ancient name of Beelzebub...in the name of Belial . . . in the name of the terrible Behemoth . . . in the cursed name of the Great Dark One . . . I call upon you in the hidden depths of the underworld. I call upon Astragoth."

As Diana watched, the figure of the tall woman seemed to waver, as though a flawed film had been drawn between them. The ugly black candle snapped and sputtered. For long seconds the only other sound in the room was the shallow, subdued breathing of the women seated at the points of the pentagram.

"I call you up to the earth, Astragoth!" Edith continued. "Through space and through time, through the ages and through the black imaginings of men I call upon you to return."

Edith's voice rose and fell in a strange rhythm. The words were English, but as Diana listened they seemed to lose their meaning and dissolve into gibberish. A blackness began to creep in around the edges of her vision. Despite her effort, she felt herself drifting away from consciousness.

It was the smell that brought her back. The haunting stink of death and decay that she had come to dread.

Diana looked around at the others. Their faces swam in and out of focus. No one moved or gave any sign they were aware of the stench. Their heads were held at odd, unnatural angles, as though they were not really looking at anything.

Then Diana looked back to the center of the pentagram, and she forgot about everything else.

Edith was there, but not as before. She was naked, her gown in a heap on the floor. Her hands were braced on the lectern, her feet planted well apart out behind her. The smooth, pale flesh of her lean body glistened with sweat. The look on her face was a wild mixture of triumph and agony.

But it was not the bizarre sight of Edith that froze Diana's heart, it was the other. There in scaly, suppurating, bestial ugliness was the creature she had seen in the fog. The thing that had emerged from the table at the séance. It stood behind the naked Edith, eyes glowing like living coals. Hands like the talons of some great bird clutched the woman's waist. A huge horny ram of a penis jutted from between the legs of the thing.

As Diana watched in horror, unable to move or speak, the creature rammed its massive rod into the anus of the red-haired woman. Diana fancied she could hear the tearing of Edith's internal organs as the beast thrust into her and withdrew, thrust again and withdrew.

Adding to the horror of the scene, Edith's face was turned toward Diana, the unblinking stare of the green eyes steadily upon her. Edith's mouth stretched wide, her tongue quivered in a silent shriek. Mucus ran from her dilated nostrils, the tendons of her throat stood out like wire rope. As Diana watched, paralyzed, a spark of red began to glow in the eyes.

Then it all vanished. Everything. Edith, the flickering candle, the silent seated women. And the beastly thing summoned from beyond this world. There was nothing. Just blackness.

And then, as suddenly, it was light again. Diana and the other four seated women looked around at each other self-consciously. In the center of the pentagram stood Edith, immaculate in her flowing gown, red hair carefully combed, smiling and pleased with herself. The overhead light was on. No candles burned.

Lisa was the first to speak. "Is that...it?"

"Yeah, where's the demon?" said Zoe.

Edith smiled at them, unperturbed. "Be serious, girls, you didn't expect an honest-to-Satan fire-breathing, pointy-tailed demon, did you?"

"I thought that was the whole idea," Harriet said.

"Well, I thought it was fun," Phyllis said. "And spooky. At least the first part. I don't remember later too well."

Edith turned to face Diana. "And how about you? What's your impression of our little game?"

Diana's mind seemed mushy, as though she were coming out of an anesthetic. There were dim, unformed impressions of something that was not pleasant, but she could not remember what it was.

"I'm—sorry," she said, "but I think I might have dozed off for a minute. I remember you pouring the...the blood on the floor, but nothing after that." As she spoke Diana looked down and saw an indistinct brown smear where the serpentine trail of red liquid had been.

"Tell the truth," Harriet said. "That wasn't real blood, was it?"

Before Edith could answer, Lisa jumped to her feet.

"Oh-oh, look at the time. It's after midnight. How in the world did we spend more than three hours down here? It seemed like only about twenty minutes."

The others checked their watches and all expressed surprise at the length of time that had passed. Diana too wondered how the fat black candle on the lectern had burned down to a puddle of wax in what seemed only minutes. She shuddered as a shadow of something obscene and evil flickered across her memory and was gone.

The women climbed the stairs from the basement, and as they emerged into the bright, cheerful kitchen their mood lightened noticeably. None of them, however, not even Harriet, had an appetite for the sandwiches.

Edith gathered their coats from the closet and handed them out. When she came to Diana she paused.

"Diana, could you stay for a bit? There's something I'd like to talk to you about."

"Harriet's riding with me tonight," Diana said.

"Harriet can ride with one of the others, can't you, Harriet?"

"Oh, sure, I can go with Zoe. Okay?"

"No problem," Zoe said.

Still Diana hesitated. "Nancy Urich is sitting with Matt, and I don't want to be too late."

"It will just be a few minutes," Edith said.

The others were edging toward the door. Diana could think of no good reason not to stay. She was not even sure why she did not want to.

"I suppose I could stay a little while," she said.

Edith smiled at her. She seemed taller, stronger. Her eyes held Diana like magnets.

"Good. I'll just say goodnight to the others, then we can talk."

Diana walked into the living room while Edith saw the other women down to their cars. She heard the doors slam and the engines start up as they drove away. Then she heard Edith's footsteps coming back up the front stairs. The tall woman came into the house and pulled the door closed behind her.

10

"Is anything wrong, Diana? You look pale."

Edith stood just inside the door with her hands on her lean hips, her shoulders thrown back. Her eyes were a smoldering green with a faint edging of red around the irises.

"I'm all right," Diana said, looking at her eyes. "Just a little shaky, I guess."

"I hope our little game tonight didn't upset you too much," Edith said. She came closer. Diana could smell her strong musky scent.

"To tell the truth, that's one game I would just as soon leave alone."

Edith gave her a slow, intimate smile. "It did get a bit heavy, didn't it?"

"You could say that."

"But don't worry, we won't be doing it again. There's no need to."

"No need?"

"We tried it once, had our fun, and that's that. Next week we can go collect shells on the beach or something."

"I think I'd like that a lot better."

"Why don't you sit down, Diana? You still look a little queasy."

Diana found the tall woman's voice strangely soothing. She realized that she truly did feel weak. She found a place on a deep-cushioned sofa. Edith sat down next to her.

"We really haven't had a chance to talk together," Edith said. "I want you to know I am sincerely glad you joined our group."

"Thank you," Diana said. "It's been excellent therapy for me."

"You're intelligent," Edith continued, "you're imaginative, you have talent, and you really are quite a beautiful woman."

Diana was embarrassed by the praise; still, she felt a little tingle of pleasure. "That's kind of you, Edith, but—"

"No, please, don't deny it," Edith interrupted. "You are an extraordinary person. There isn't anything wrong with a woman admiring the intelligence and the beauty of another woman, is there?"

"No, of course there isn't."

"I'm glad to hear you say that. But after all, you are an artist. You would not be held back by silly conventions from giving free expression to your admiration...or love."

Diana felt her face grow warm. She tried to toss off a light laugh, but it didn't quite work. She said, "I don't know about all that free expression. In many ways I'm a pretty conventional person."

Edith placed a hand on her arm. "Ah, but I'll bet you're not afraid to try something new and different, just because it *is* new to you."

"I—I suppose that's true."

Edith's face was very close to hers now. Diana admired the classic high cheekbones, the delicately arched nose. The hot green eyes with their faint red haloes held her.

"I wonder what you would say if I asked you to try something new right now?" Edith's voice was low and husky, her tone a caress.

"I guess that would depend on what it was." Diana's throat was dry. She felt a hot surge of excitement, but somewhere deep within her was revulsion.

Edith's hand had moved from Diana's arm to her leg. Diana could feel the heat of it through the thin cotton slacks. Ever so gently the fingers began to knead the flesh of her thigh.

"I think you know what I'm talking about." The tall woman's voice dropped to a whisper. Diana felt the moist breath on her cheek.

"I'm not that way," Diana said. She was surprised at the lack of conviction she heard in her own voice. The strength seemed to be flowing out of her body, and the sensation was not at all unpleasant.

"How can you or I or any of us know the way we really are?" Edith went on in the seductive whisper. "The only thing we can do is give ourselves the chance for new experiences, new forms of expression. You, as an artist, must understand that."

Edith's hand moved up the inside of Diana's thigh toward her crotch. The strong fingers seemed to sear Diana's flesh, but a part of her mind did not want the other woman to stop.

"I can't," she said. "I must not."

Edith's lips brushed her cheek lightly as a shadow. "Oh, but you can, Diana. You know you can."

Diana felt herself go moist between the legs. "Please don't," she said.

"Tell the truth, you want me to, don't you? You want me to touch you." The red-haired woman's lips were against the corner of Diana's mouth. Her tongue dampened Diana's lips. "You want me to taste you. You want to taste me."

86

Diana found she could not speak. She rolled her head from side to side. Edith's tongue traced a wet path on her cheek.

"You do, don't you?" said the purring, coaxing voice. "You would like to kiss me right now. You would like to wash my body with your tongue. You want to put it into me while I taste you right...*here.*"

Edith's fingers found the swelling of her vulva and pressed against the yielding lips.

"No!" Diana struggled for control of herself. She grasped the other woman's wrist, but found she had neither the strength nor the will to pull her hand away.

Edith's mouth stretched into a smile of triumph.

"Mommy!"

Little Timmy Werhaus stood in the archway between the living room and the stairway to the second floor. His eyes were wide, his tiny fists pressed to his mouth.

Edith snatched her hand away and whirled on the boy. "What are you doing here?"

"I'm afraid!"

With Edith distracted for a moment, Diana recovered her power of movement. She got to her feet and started for the door. Edith turned the full force of her anger on the little boy.

"Damn you! I told you to stay in bed!"

The voice that came out of Edith's mouth was rough-edged and guttural, like no voice Diana had heard before.

"I've got to leave, Edith," she said.

"No!" For a moment the red-haired woman seemed confused, her attention switching between Diana and the boy. "Go, then," she said suddenly in a near snarl.

Diana hesitated at the door, looking back at Timmy. The child stood in the archway exactly as he had when he first spoke.

"Well? What are you waiting for?" Edith demanded.

Feeling her own anger growing, Diana left the house before she could become involved in an ugly scene with Edith.

When the two of them were alone, Edith again turned on the boy.

"You...little...bastard!" Edith spat the words out like bullets. "You ruined everything."

Timmy's eyes grew wide as Edith advanced on him. "Who are you? You're not my mommy. Where's my mommy?"

Edith's face froze. "You want to see your mommy, do you? Your mommy's out in the kitchen." She put out a hand. "Come along, I'll take you to her."

The boy shrank from her. "No, I don't want to go with you. I don't like you."

Edith's long fingers closed over the child's arm. "Come along," she said.

Timmy screamed. Edith paid no attention. With no effort she pulled him along with her into the kitchen. She held him with one hand while she slid open the drawer where the knives were kept.

11

Philip Werhaus came home at ten o'clock on Sunday morning. He pulled the Caddy up behind the garage, got out, stretched, and rubbed his eyes. He was glad to be home. He never slept well in a motel bed. Had Edith not said she was having her women friends over last night, he might have tried to make the late drive from Los Angeles. However, he liked to give her the freedom to pursue her hobbies, and he got the impression from her that his presence last night would have put a damper on the proceedings, whatever they were this time.

He pulled open the garage door and drove the Caddy in next to Edith's station wagon. He came back out to the street and lowered the garage door. The breeze was fresh off the ocean, salty and cool. Philip drew a deep breath and thought, as he often did, how lucky he was to live here in Tranquilo Beach and not in crowded, polluted Los Angeles.

He started up the steps to the front door, counting himself an all-round lucky man. He could not ask for a better family—beautiful, imaginative Edith, and sturdy little Timmy with the smile that could melt his heart. Philip had been over forty when Timmy was born, and not very enthusiastic at the time. But like so many men to whom fatherhood comes late, he now thought Timmy was the greatest thing that had ever happened to him.

He pushed open the front door and walked in.

Edith was sitting in a chair by the window waiting for him. She wore a form-fitting long dress of yellow satin that was slit to the thigh on one side. Framed in the window, her red hair loose about her shoulders, she made a beautiful picture. Philip stopped and caught his breath, admiring the way she looked. Edith rose gracefully from the chair, floated into his arms, and kissed him with excessive passion.

Philip drew back and looked at her. "Hey, what's the occasion?"

"What do you mean?" Her green eyes, almost on a level with his, danced mischievously. Some trick of the sunlight gave iridescent red rims to the irises.

"That dress," Philip said. "That kiss. I've only been away one night. You make me feel like Rhett Butler home from the war."

"Is there anything wrong with that?"

"Well, no, not *wrong* ..."

"I missed you, that's all," she said in a soft, purring voice. "I want to show you how much."

Philip stared at his wife and wondered at the difference he saw in her this morning. He had always been proud of her—the beautiful hair, the dramatic facial bones, the way she commanded attention everywhere she went. A quiet man himself, nothing special to look at with his myopic vision and thinning hair, Philip was always content to stand aside and let Edith take center stage, secure in the knowledge that later she would be his alone. But never, in the fourteen years of their marriage, had he seen the sexual, animal side of her that he saw now.

Edith moved closer and ground the lower part of her

90

body against him suggestively. He felt the stirring of an erection, and was unaccountably embarrassed.

"How about it?" Edith said, her voice a soft growl in his ear. "Want to go upstairs and get fucked?"

Philip reacted as though she had dashed a glass of cold water in his face. Edith Werhaus, flamboyant and liberated though she was, simply did not use that word. Philip disengaged himself from her arms and stepped back. He laughed nervously.

"At least let me wash up a little first."

"Don't wash up for my sake," she said, lips twisting in a lascivious smile. "I like it dirty."

"No, really, I'll feel better if I take a quick wash."

Philip escaped to the bathroom. He took off his glasses, cleaned them with toilet paper, and put them on again. He leaned close to the mirror. Aside from a slight flush to his cheeks, which he was sure had just come up, there was nothing new in the way he looked that might have triggered Edith's strange behavior. In the past her sex drive had always been somewhat below normal, if there was a normal. This had suited Philip, as it matched his own appetites. A quiet coupling two or three times a week had been plenty for both of them. Neither of them ever spoke about it before or after, they just did it, then went to sleep. But this...Edith was like a different woman. Philip could not decide whether he was more excited or frightened.

He quickly scrubbed his hands and face, then held the cold washcloth against the back of his neck. He would have liked to take a full shower, but he could sense Edith's presence outside the door, and he did not want to keep her waiting.

When he came out she was leaning in the hallway arch, one hip shot forward so much of the long, slim leg was visible through the slit in the dress.

"Ready now?" she asked, running her eyes hungrily over his body.

"I, uh, think I need a drink of cold water." He smiled at her quickly and went into the kitchen. He let the cold water run for a minute before he held a glass under the tap. The kitchen floor, he noted, was freshly mopped. Unusual, since Edith usually did that on Monday. Looking closer, he saw only a part of the floor had been cleaned. Something spilled, probably. Still, it was unlike Edith not to finish the job.

"Are you going to drink that straight, or would you like some whiskey in it?"

Philip started. He had been staring at the floor and had not seen Edith come into the room.

"No, thanks," he said, "I'm not much of a morning drinker." He swallowed half the water from the glass, poured the rest into the sink, and set the glass down.

"Now," Edith said pointedly, "is there anything else you have to do before we fuck?"

He flinched at hearing the word again, and tried to cover it up with a little shrug. "No, there's nothing else I have to do."

Edith planted her feet apart so one bare leg was thrust completely through the slit of the dress. She beckoned to him with both hands. "Come and get it, lover."

Still Philip hesitated. He looked around, unable to lose the feeling that something was very wrong here.

"Where's Timmy?"

"Sonofabitch!" Edith's anger flared. "He isn't going to bother us."

"But he always likes to meet me when I come home," Philip persisted.

"He's outside playing. Now are you going to take me to bed or do I have to fuck a broom handle?"

"Why are you talking like that, Edith?"

She softened her tone suddenly and held out her hands to him. "I'll talk any way you want me to, darling."

Philip walked across the scrubbed portion of the kitchen to join his wife. He had an eerie sensation that he was walking into another world.

When he reached her, Edith pulled his head forward and kissed him. Her tongue, hot and quivering like a small wet animal, probed deep into his mouth.

"Come upstairs with me, Philip," she said with her lips still on him. "I want it now."

"Yes, all right," he said, feeling awkward as an adolescent on his first date. They went up together to their bedroom, and as Philip undressed he wondered about his ability to perform under stress. He began formulating an excuse in case he should be impotent.

He need not have worried. As soon as he was naked Edith was all over him. She bore him down onto the bed, ignoring his half-joking protests. With her fingers, her tongue, her teeth, she explored parts of his body no one had ever touched. Instantly he had an erection stiff as a baton. Edith stroked him, prodded him, pinched him, nipped him until his body cried out for release.

She pinned his shoulders to the mattress with her knees and thrust her belly forward, bringing the wet joining of her legs down over his face. He inhaled the feral scent of her and strained forward to taste her. Laughing, taunting, she pulled away an instant before his tongue found her.

For the next thirty minutes Edith played with him. She taught him moves and positions he had never imagined in his most erotic fantasies. The pleasure increased to a point of unbearable tension. Time and again she brought him to within a heartbeat of orgasm, only to stop and pull him back. The thinking part of his mind demanded to know where this woman, his wife, had learned these delicious acts of obscenity. The feeling part of his mind cried, *Don't stop!*

Finally his body could stand no more. He grasped Edith's shoulders and tried to ease her down on her back.

"No," she growled. "This time you will be on the bottom." With a strength that surprised him, she pushed him flat against the mattress and raised her lean, glistening body over his. Then, a centimeter at a time, she lowered herself, taking his stiff, aching organ inside her.

The sensation was utterly unlike anything Philip had ever experienced. Slowly, sensually, Edith began to ride up and down on his penis. She made little moaning growls that were punctuated by the wet smack of flesh on flesh. Gradually she increased the rhythm, staying in perfect synchronization with Philip's straining thrusts. At the precise moment when he could not have stood one more second without release, she dropped her full weight on him, her wet buttocks slapping against his pelvis.

There was one flash of ecstatic pleasure for Philip Werhaus, then unspeakable agony as he saw what was happening to him. The face above him wavered and dissolved. Then it was not the high-cheeked patrician beauty of Edith that hovered there, but a creature of indescribable horror. The dim red glow of its eyes intensified until they were like twin lasers burning into Philip's brain. Into his soul. It was at that moment that he understood how dreadfully he was being violated. His was the body that was being entered. His bowels tore and bled as he shrieked unheard. Everything inside him exploded.

*   *   *

94

Later, the thing that now wore Philip's body looked down at the used-up husk of a woman lying dead beside him in the bed. The lips that had been Philip's stretched in an ugly smile. Behind the brown irises, the eyes glowed red.

12

The week that followed the Saturday-night meeting at Edith's house went swiftly for Diana. Monday was the Fourth of July, and Kirby Franklin took her and Matt to Oceanside for the parade. That night they watched the fireworks shot off over the ocean from the Tranquilo Beach pier. On Wednesday they had barbecued hamburgers in the backyard of the cottage. Friday night she and Kirby went to a movie in San Clemente. The tall newspaperman was becoming an important part of her life, yet something made her pull back whenever the relationship threatened to become truly intimate.

On Sunday Diana was half regretting she had agreed to see Kirby that night. She was not in the mood to go out. Troubling her were the blank spots in her memory of Saturday. It had no form, but lurking just outside her consciousness was something she did not want to face.

Diana's work had suffered too since that night. Her current project was to do illustrations for a children's book called *Dr. Nose,* a clever parody of the James Bond genre that grownups could enjoy with their children. She was trying to paint a comical monster created by the bumbling doctor, but since Saturday night she had been unable to set down a single brushstroke that looked right.

Now Harriet Nagle was on the phone, adding to Diana's overall uneasiness.

"Nobody has seen hide nor hair of Edith all week," Harriet announced.

Diana's fingers tightened around the receiver. "Not since the Saturday night we were all out at her place."

"You got it. Both Lisa and Phyllis have tried to call her, but got no answer."

"That's funny," Diana said. She had not told anyone about what had happened between Edith and her after the others left. She told herself it had just been some weird impulse of Edith's, probably brought on by the bizarre doings in the rec room. Now she was beginning to have doubts, but she was still not ready to discuss it with Harriet.

"I called her again this morning and Philip answered," Harriet continued.

"Well, why didn't you say so?"

"I was getting to it."

"Did he tell you where Edith is?"

"According to Philip, she went back to visit her sister in Boston and took Timmy with her."

"Well, that explains it then," Diana said.

"Not to me it doesn't."

"What do you mean?"

"It means I don't believe him. I've known Edith Werhaus for a good many years, and I never heard her mention any sister in Boston."

"That doesn't mean she doesn't have one."

"I'd be willing to bet money on it."

"But why would Philip lie to you?" Diana asked.

"What I think is that they had a fight. Edith packed her bags, put Timmy in the car, and took off."

It was possible, Diana thought. If Edith was still in

her strange mood when Philip came home, it could have triggered a quarrel. She said, "Still, it's funny she wouldn't tell anyone."

"No, that would be like Edith. If there is anything less than perfect about her marriage or her child or her husband or her life, you would never hear about it from her."

"I guess it is her business, after all."

"It's just that she kind of left us in the lurch. The group, I mean. Without Edith here to take charge, nobody seems to want to get anything going."

If that was an invitation for her to take charge, Diana chose not to recognize it. She said, "We'll have to get together one day soon. Right now I have to go to work."

Harriet's voice chilled suddenly. "Oh, I'm sorry. I didn't know I was interrupting. Talk to you another time."

Diana gently replaced the receiver. She did not want to hurt Harriet's feelings, but she simply did not feel like chattering the morning away. She would make it up to Harriet later. As for the others, Diana had no desire to see them again this soon. The bad taste from the night at Edith's was still too much with her.

She returned to her illustration for the children's book, but by two in the afternoon she still had nothing but meaningless blobs of color. She drank a glass of wine and played a favorite record, Vivaldi's *The Four Seasons,* which usually primed her creative pump, but today she got nothing but a small headache. She lay down to try to take a nap, and before she was ready, it was seven o'clock and Kirby was there with the sitter, Nancy Urich.

She tried to keep the irrational irritation out of her voice when she spoke to him. "Kirby, I've had a really

98

frustrating day. Would you mind very much if we didn't go out tonight?"

"More problems with drawing the lovable monster?" he asked.

She nodded. "That, and other things."

"Best thing in the world for you is to get out. Have a good dinner, nice bottle of wine, witty conversation. You'll feel a hundred percent better."

"Well, I don't know. I haven't fed Matt."

"I can make dinner for him, Mrs. Cross," Nancy said. "I know where everything is."

"There, you see?" Kirby said. "There's no excuse for you to stay home. Throw on something sexy and let's go."

"I have to take a shower first."

"So take one. Our dinner reservation isn't until eight o'clock."

Diana drew an exasperated sigh. Unable to think of any more arguments, she trudged off to the shower.

Dinner that night at the Breakers Restaurant south of town was less than successful. At the beginning Kirby was witty and affectionate, as always, but Diana was unable to respond. By the time dessert came he had sunk into a noncommunicative sulk to match her own. Diana tried then to lighten the mood, but it was too late. Her heart was not in it, and Kirby knew it. He called for the check even before they had finished their coffee, and it was with a sense of relief that they left the restaurant and got into his car for the ten-minute drive to Diana's cottage.

When they reached her door Kirby kissed her automatically and suddenly it was as though a dam had broken inside her. All at once she realized how much she wanted this man close to her, and how childishly she had been acting all evening. She responded to his kiss with a fervor that surprised both of them.

"Want to come in?" she said.

He looked at her curiously. "Sure."

They went inside and found Nancy Urich in the big chair with her feet tucked under her, reading a paperback book that detailed the peculiar sex life of a recently deceased movie star. She marked her place in the book and smiled at them when they entered.

"Any problems?" Diana asked her.

"Nope. Matt didn't want to eat his asparagus, but I can't really blame him for that. We finally compromised so he ate half of it and got a dish of ice cream. He's been asleep now for an hour."

"Thanks, Nancy." Diana took the bills from her wallet and paid the girl for the evening. It was something she always insisted on. No militant feminist, Diana still felt it was the woman's obligation to pay for the baby-sitter when the man paid for the evening out.

"Goodnight, Mrs. Cross. Mr. Franklin." Nancy started for the door.

"Do you need a ride home?" Kirby asked, without a lot of enthusiasm.

"What for? It's only a five-minute walk."

Diana smiled. In many parts of Los Angeles a five-minute walk after dark was like a stroll through the jungle. Here in Tranquilo Beach violent crime was something you watched on television.

Nancy went out and closed the door. Kirby and Diana stood for a moment looking at each other. Then he took her in his arms. They kissed long and deep. Diana's body responded to his more fiercely than ever before. It was as though she needed his physical touch to wipe away the bad feelings of the past week.

Kirby pulled her head against his chest. He said, "I want to stay with you tonight."

She held him tightly, feeling the play of his back muscles under the lightweight sport jacket he wore. "And I want you to stay, darling."

He started to move with her toward the bedroom.

Diana held back. "But we can't."

He looked down at her, frowning. "We can't? Why the hell can't we?"

"Because of Matt."

"He's asleep."

"He could wake up."

"We'll lock the door."

"He'll still know we're in there."

Kirby began to grow angry. "Well, what if he does? It's not like we're asking him to participate."

"There's no need to be crude."

He stepped back and looked at her appraisingly. "The problem really isn't Matt, is it?"

"I just don't want to do it this way, Kirby."

"I'm beginning to think you don't want to do it *any* way."

She reached out for him. "That isn't fair."

He took hold of her wrists and put her arms back at her sides. "You always have some reason why we can't go to my place, you think a motel is too unromantic, and we can't do it here because Matt's in the house. Tell me, Diana, do you have something against sex?"

"God, that's always the bottom line, isn't it? Anytime a woman doesn't dive into the sack as soon as the man starts breathing heavy, she must be frigid. Or a lesbian. Jesus!"

"Come off it, Diana. We've been seeing each other two or three nights a week now for almost a month. I wouldn't call that exactly diving into the sack. Sex is a perfectly natural act between men and women who care for each other. I thought you and I fit into that category."

Diana spun away from him. "I don't want to talk about it any more."

"Good enough." Kirby walked out the door, closing it behind him just a little more forcefully than necessary.

Diana stood for a minute in the center of the living room, chewing on a knuckle. Then she crossed the room quickly and dropped into the chair where Nancy had been sitting.

What the hell am I doing? she asked herself silently. She lit a cigarette. Kirby Franklin was the first man to really arouse her since the divorce from Jerry. Kirby was intelligent, gentle, witty, loving, and—admit it—sexy as hell. She wanted him in bed, no two ways about that. Why, then, did she act like some candy-ass virgin when the subject came up? Her concern for Matt was part of it, that was true. But, as Kirby pointed out, she could not blame the boy for her reluctance to go to a motel, or to Kirby's place. Was she afraid to make a commitment? That was bullshit. Without commitment life was a shallow make-believe. She was ready for a man, and she knew it. She was ready for Kirby Franklin. Diana stared at the closed front door and willed him to return.

The doorbell rang.

With a glad cry, Diana jumped up and skipped across the room. She pulled open the door, and the greeting she had ready died on her lips.

At first she did not recognize Philip Werhaus. She had met him only twice, briefly, at Edith's, and she had not seen him without his glasses before. When recognition came, she could not fully conceal her disappointment.

"Oh, hello, Philip."

"Hi, Diana. Are you busy?"

"Well, no. I mean, I just got in."

"I—I wonder if I can come in for a minute."

"Well...all right." Diana stood aside as he came into the living room. He seemed different tonight. His voice was stronger, his movements more decisive, although his words were innocuous enough.

"I don't want to be any bother," Philip said. "It's just that I've been feeling lonely and kind of down since Edith left, and I'd like to talk to someone."

Immediately Diana felt sorry for him. Poor, bland Philip Werhaus was out of his league with a woman as overpowering as Edith.

"Sit down, Philip. Can I get you something?"

"No, no thanks, I don't want to be any bother."

"A cup of coffee? It's instant."

"That'll be fine."

Diana went out to the compact kitchen and put a pan of water on the gas flame to heat. She spooned coffee crystals into two cups. She did not mind talking to Philip Werhaus for a little while, but she hoped he was not going to dump a load of troubles on her. She had plenty of her own. Immediately she was ashamed of herself. The man was clearly hurting, and if talking about it would make him feel better, it was a small enough sacrifice for her to make.

She poured the boiling water into the cups and carried them back into the living room.

"Do you take anything in yours?" she asked.

"No, thanks, black is fine."

Diana handed him the cup, then sat across from him on the sofa. Philip immediately got up from his chair and came over to sit beside her. It made her uncomfortable, but there was no way she could move now without seeming to reject his friendship. She settled herself gingerly, careful not to let their knees touch.

"Edith thought a lot of you, Diana."

103

She looked at him closely. The strangeness in his voice was more evident.

"She said several times that you were a very beautiful woman. She was right."

"Well...thank you, Philip." Diana was acutely embarrassed by the clumsy flattery.

"A beautiful, intelligent woman like you really shouldn't be without a man," he said.

She tried to toss it off lightly. "Oh, I don't know about that. There are a lot of disadvantages to having a man around the house all the time."

She pretended to see something on the other side of the room, and started to rise. Philip's hand on her thigh, surprisingly strong, kept her from rising.

"A woman like you is not complete without a man," he said. "A man who knows how to make you happy."

Diana stared down at the hand that was rubbing her leg. She looked up into the man's face.

"Philip, what are you doing?"

"I know how to make you happy, Diana." His voice was almost unrecognizable now. "Let me show you."

His lips stretched into a smile that was like nothing she had ever seen on Philip's face. She was drawn to the eyes. Around the edges of the irises there was a faint reddish glow.

13

When he slammed out of Diana's cottage Kirby Franklin was mad. He was mad at Diana for the I-want-to-but-we-mustn't song and dance she was giving him about going to bed. Worse, he was mad at himself for coming on like some horny high school kid.

He got into his car and drove north along the old Coast Highway to a viewpoint turnoff. In years past it had been a favorite makeout spot for the local teenagers. Modern teenagers were much too sophisticated to do it in a cramped automobile. They all had vans with waterbeds in the back, stereophonic sound, and a light show.

A fat pale moon rode low over the ocean, laying down a sparkly path on the dark water. A lover's moon, for sure. Probably everybody in Southern California was getting laid tonight except Kirby Franklin, he reflected.

But enough of this kvetching, he told himself. His life in Tranquilo Beach was good, overall. He enjoyed editing the *Tide,* and wouldn't mind if that's what he did for the rest of his life. The newspaper was owned by a millionaire developer who lived up the coast in Laguna Beach. The man kept the paper as a hobby and as a tax write-off, and didn't care if the little weekly made money or not. As long as Kirby worked in the names of the owner's friends and the owner's wife's friends often enough, he could do whatever else he wanted to with the paper.

For Kirby the relaxed atmosphere of running a weekly in a beach town was heaven. A graduate of the University of Missouri, he'd learned his trade in the pressure cooker of St. Louis journalism. As a reporter for the *Globe-Democrat,* Kirby was always under the lash to keep pace with the more prestigious *Post-Dispatch.*

The constant pressure wore Kirby down physically and spiritually until he either had to get out of St. Louis or check into a rest home. His young wife at the time was born and raised in St. Louis, and she would not hear of leaving. As she saw it, Kirby's only problem was that he lacked the drive to succeed. She let him know that if he left St. Louis he would be leaving alone. That afternoon Kirby quit his job at the *Globe-Democrat,* said goodbye to wife and city and headed for California.

He found a job with the Long Beach *Independent,* and stayed there two years while his nerves calmed and he brought his weight back up to where it should be. Then he heard about the opening for an editor of the *Tide.* He drove down for an interview and was hired on the spot.

In the five years in Tranquilo Beach Kirby had done stories on surfing competition, the grunion run, the annual art festival, class reunions, civic clubs, and the Christmas regatta. He had editorialized against littering the beach, lowering the drinking age, and raising the beach parking fee. He had been for brighter streetlights, improved sewers, and a new car for the police force. On the rare occasions when he grew nostalgic about the excitement of big-city journalism he had only to compare his new freedom and relaxed pace to those frenzied years in St. Louis.

It was true that he might have wished for a livelier social life. There were not a lot of eligible women in Tranquilo Beach, and he knew enough not to get mixed up with the female tourists. There had been women in his life, of course, but none he would have considered for a permanent relationship. Not until Diana Cross. For the first time in seven years he was thinking it might be nice to be a part of a marriage again. But before that line of thinking went any further, they would have to straighten out this sex thing.

Sitting there in his car looking out over the ocean, he made a decision. Stomping off to sulk like some fuzzy-cheeked adolescent was no way to handle this. He would go back and sit down with Diana and they would talk this thing out. It was time to find out if this relationship was going anywhere, or whether they ought to call the whole thing off now.

Kirby cranked the engine to life, backed out onto the highway, and headed the car back toward the sleeping town.

The sudden ring of the doorbell startled both of them. Philip Werhaus snatched his hand away from Diana's leg and spun around toward the door. Diana, no longer held on the sofa by the pressure of his hand, sprang to her feet. She hurried across the room and threw open the door. Her knees went weak with relief when she saw Kirby Franklin standing there.

"Kirby, I'm so glad you came back!"

He reacted with surprise to the greeting, then looked past Diana at Philip Werhaus, who had risen and was standing by the sofa.

"Am I interrupting something?"

"God, no, Kirby. Please come in."

Diana stepped to one side and Kirby entered the living room.

"Hello, Kirby," Philip said. There was no warmth in his tone.

Kirby looked him over curiously. "Hi."

"Philip was just leaving," Diana said.

The two men faced each other. Philip seemed undecided about what to do. When he turned to Diana his angry look was far out of proportion to the situation.

"Goodnight," he muttered, and stalked out the door that Diana still held open. She closed it firmly behind him.

"What was that all about?" Kirby asked when he and Diana were alone.

"I'm darned if I know," Diana said. "Philip came over right after you left and said he wanted to talk. He looked so sad that I felt sorry for him and told him to come in. I made some coffee and we sat down, and right away he started acting funny."

"Funny in what way?" Kirby asked.

"He started in telling me how I'm a beautiful woman, and I needed a man, and all that crap. He put his hand on my leg—he's stronger than you'd think—and I was really starting to get worried. That's when you came back, thank God."

"He was really trying to put the moves on you?"

"That's sure what it seemed like."

Kirby looked thoughtful. "That doesn't sound like the Philip Werhaus I know."

"You and me both, but that's what happened," Diana said.

"Do you have any idea why?"

"Who knows? Maybe he came unglued when Edith took the boy and walked out on him."

"I heard they went back east to visit Edith's sister," Kirby said.

"That's the story Philip is telling people, but Harriet Nagle thinks they had a fight and Edith moved out. From the way Philip was acting tonight, I'm inclined to believe her."

Kirby looked toward the door where Philip had gone out. "Maybe I'd better go after him."

Diana put a hand on his arm. "Please, Kirby, I don't want you to go right now."

"Anyway, I'm glad I came back."

"So am I," Diana said with feeling. "Why *did* you come back?"

"I got to thinking that we were acting childish, and that we ought to talk about it."

"I think that's a good idea, but I'm really not up to it tonight. Could we talk in the morning?"

"You want me to come back then?"

"No. We can talk about it before you go home."

"Do you mean that?"

"I mean it. I need you here with me tonight, Kirby."

He inclined his head toward the back bedroom. "What about Matt?"

"He's a sound sleeper."

After a moment Kirby said, "You talked me into it."

It was Diana who snapped off the light and led the way back to her room.

14

The two boys stood at the bottom of the steps and looked up at the forbidding stone house. A black-and-white dog frolicked at their feet, urging them on to adventure of some sort.

The smaller of the two boys was Kevin. He wore glasses, which gave him the look of a friendly young owl. He said, "I wish I lived there. Timmy's really lucky."

Wade was a head taller and six months older than Kevin, and was good at all kinds of sports. He said, "Oh, I don't know. My brother says it's haunted."

"Aww, there's no such things as ghosts," Kevin said.

"Oh yeah? You think you know more than my brother? He's in high school."

"People don't really live in haunted houses," Kevin persisted. "Anyway, Timmy never said anything about any ghosts, and he'd know, wouldn't he?"

"Okay, then, if you're so smart, where *is* Timmy? I haven't seen him for a week."

"Well, neither have I," Kevin admitted.

Wade pressed his point. "He didn't even come down to the pier for the fireworks last week. Everybody comes down to the pier on the Fourth of July. What do you say about that?"

Kevin shrugged under the weight of the older boy's logic.

"We could go up and ring the doorbell," Wade suggested.

"What if Timmy's mother comes to the door?"

"What if she does? You're not afraid of Timmy's mother, are you?"

"No way. It's just that she's...kind of weird."

"Aah, *you're* weird. Come on, unless you're chicken."

With obvious reluctance Kevin climbed the stone steps with his friend while the dog bounded joyously ahead of them. They stopped at the front door and looked at each other uncertainly. Then Wade, recognizing his responsibility, jabbed at the doorbell button. He pulled his finger back quickly, as though he expected an electrical shock.

The boys could hear clearly the peal of the chimes inside the house. They waited, glancing around nervously and edging back away from the door in case it should fly open suddenly.

"Nobody's home," said Kevin, pushing the glasses back up on the thin bridge of his nose. "Let's go."

"No, wait a minute," said Wade. "Look how all the blinds are pulled down on the windows."

"What of it?"

"If you had nice big windows in your house to look out at the ocean, would you pull all the blinds down so you couldn't see out?"

"I don't know. Let's go."

"What's your hurry? Let's go take a look around in back."

"What if we get caught?"

"There's nobody home, you said so yourself. And if anybody does ask, we're just looking for Timmy. Nothing wrong with that, is there?"

"Well...okay."

With Wade leading the way, the two boys rounded the corner of the big house and walked along the side wall, where a laurel hedge grew, to the backyard. The dog raced ahead of them, then rushed back, beside himself with excitement.

The yard behind the house contained a lemon tree and an apricot tree. It sloped gently up and away from the house to where a redwood fence held out the scrub oak and palmetto that grew on the hillside. The grass of the lawn was healthy green, but it crunched slightly under the boys tennis shoes, showing it needed water.

Bright lawn furniture of aluminum and plastic was set out as though the people would be there any minute. Along the rear of the house were flower beds, all carefully tended, except for a large patch near the far corner where the earth had been freshly turned.

"Come on, Wade, let's go," said the smaller boy. "There's nothing back here."

The dog was systematically checking out the area for evidence of previous dog visits. He sniffed at the trees, the bushes, the furniture, and ritually lifted his leg at each.

Wade looked around the yard, hoping to see something that would justify his idea to come back here, but it was just a yard. He was about to give up and start back when Kevin clutched at his sleeve.

"Wade, look at Max."

The dog had prowled the length of the flower beds and stopped at the patch of raw earth at the far end. There he stopped and cocked his head as though listening. He barked twice—short, sharp exclamations— then he began to dig.

"Cut it out, Max," the taller boy called.

"What's he doing?" Kevin said.

"He's got a gopher or something. Or he thinks he has."

"Let's go see," said Kevin, forgetting for the moment his desire to leave.

The boys walked over to where the dog was eagerly scooping the earth out with his forepaws. As they stood watching, he uncovered a pale object clotted with dirt.

Kevin made a face. "Is it a gopher?"

"I can't tell," Wade said.

Max seized the partially uncovered prize in his teeth and braced his legs, ready to pull whatever it was out of the ground. When it came easily away from the earth, the dog stumbled backward and looked up at the boys with the thing still in his mouth.

"What *is* it, anyway?" Kevin asked.

Kevin squatted and held out his hand. "Come here, Max. Give it to me."

The dog danced backward, wagging his tail and shaking the thing he held in his mouth. Wade darted forward and grasped the dog's collar. With his free hand he took hold of the pale thing clamped in Max's jaws and started to pull it free. Abruptly he snatched his hand away and stumbled to his feet.

"Jesus, let's get out of here!"

"What's the matter?" Kevin asked, but his friend was already running, so the smaller boy took off after him.

The dog hesitated, wondering if this was part of the game. When he realized the boys were not playing, that they were running away and leaving him, he dropped his prize and followed.

It lay there on the grass after they had gone, palm up as though in supplication. A child's hand.

15

The Bayview Hospital in Tranquilo Beach was small and modern, set well back on a stretch of green lawn on the southern edge of the town. Its facilities were limited, but they had always met the needs of the community. Because there was so little demand, Bayview was not equipped for the performance of complete autopsies. Nor was there a full-time pathologist on the staff. That was why Dr. Ira Sussman from Oceanside General Hospital had been sent for to examine the grisly find from the Werhaus backyard.

The standby operating room at Bayview was serving as an autopsy lab on this Monday morning. Present along with Dr. Sussman were Bo Ratcher, chief of the tiny Tranquilo Beach police force, and Kirby Franklin. Kirby was there officially as a representative of the media, but unofficially because he was a poker-playing friend of Chief Ratcher.

The body of Edith Werhaus, opened down the middle and with the top of the skull removed, lay on the bare operating table. The remains of Timmy Werhaus were arranged on a second table that had been wheeled into the room. The pathologist, a bright, birdlike little man, scurried between the two tables prodding here, slicing there. The other men stood back at a respectful distance.

Dr. Sussman straightened up finally and looked at Ratcher and Kirby Franklin. He spoke with a faint German accent. "I suppose you want to know how long they have been dead. Police always want to know that first."

"It's helpful," Ratcher said. "Can you tell?"

"From the extent of decomposition I would say a week. Perhaps as much as two weeks. An analysis of the stomach contents will tell us more."

"Did they die at the same time?" Ratcher asked.

"Close. It would be a reasonable assumption."

"What was the cause of death?" Kirby asked. He tried not to look directly at what lay on the tables.

"For the little boy it is easy to say. Multiple stab wounds. Whoever did it apparently wanted it to last a long time."

Chief Ratcher was a heavy man who perspired freely, especially in times of stress. Now, despite the cool temperature in the operating room, his blue uniform shirt was soaked through in the back and under the arms.

"Was the boy still alive when they...cut him to pieces like that?" the chief asked.

"At least at the start, I would say. It is likely he fainted long before it was over."

"God, I hope so," the policeman muttered.

"What about the woman?" Kirby asked. "What killed her?"

"That one is not so easy," said Dr. Sussman. "Except for a clean, dressed wound on the inner forearm, there are no apparent external injuries. However, the internal organs have been severely traumatized." He held up a misshapen splotchy brown object. "Look at this liver."

"Looks sick," Kirby said.

"No one could live with a liver like this. Additionally, there is evidence of some kind of corrosive brain damage."

"How are these things possible without some external signs?" Kirby asked.

"That I cannot answer. Possibly it is some virulent disease. It is like nothing I have seen before."

"This is a hell of a thing," Chief Ratcher said. "A hell of a thing."

Sussman cocked his head and peered at the police chief. "You don't have a lot of homicides up here, do you?"

"If you don't count traffic deaths, this makes two in the last twenty-five years. The other one was when Maury Bates shotgunned a San Francisco hippie who fed his daughter LSD and knocked her up. That one went down as manslaughter and Maury got off with probation. But this...this is something else."

"I don't presume to tell you your business, Chief Ratcher," said the doctor, "but if I were you, I know who I would be looking for."

"That's easy," Ratcher said. "The husband. I called his office in L.A. They said he hasn't been in for a week. Nobody's heard from him."

"That doesn't look good," Sussman commented.

"I know it, but it's still hard for me to believe. Hell, I've known Phil Werhaus ever since he moved to T-Beach. He's always been a soft-spoken, mild guy who wouldn't step on an ant if he could avoid it."

"They always are," the pathologist observed.

Ratcher shook his head sadly. "You just never know about people."

"I saw Philip Werhaus just last night," Kirby said. "He wasn't so soft-spoken and mild then."

"What do you mean?"

"He was trying to proposition Diana Cross."

"That's the divorcée with the little boy who moved into the Thompsons' cottage?"

Kirby nodded.

Ratcher pulled out a handkerchief and mopped perspiration from his neck. "It's harder than hell to believe something like that about a man you've known for years."

"It happens all the time," Sussman said. "Honor student, Eagle Scout, parents' pride and joy. One day he picks up a rifle and walks into a crowd shooting. I have yet to hear a good explanation for why this is."

"Is there any possibility that dope is involved in this case?" Kirby asked.

"That is a good question," said the doctor. "However, there are no external signs on the bodies that either used narcotics. Again, we will have to wait for a more thorough autopsy."

"Knowing how straight Phil Werhaus has always been, I can't imagine him involved in dope," Ratcher said.

"It's a possibility you should not ignore," said Sussman.

"I'm not ignoring anything. I have a scientific team coming from the sheriff's office to go through the house." He consulted a watch. "I should be getting over there to meet them."

"Okay if I come along?" Kirby asked.

"It's all right with me, Kirby," Ratcher said, "but with the courts the way they are today, you know how careful we have to be about gathering evidence."

"Don't worry, I'll stay well out of the way," Kirby said. "And I promise not to touch anything until the sheriff's team is finished with it."

"We'd better get going then," said the chief. "I want to be there when they arrive."

Dr. Sussman waved an arm at the two bodies. "I'll

need these sent down to Oceanside if you want me to do a tissue analysis. All my equipment is there."

"I'll have somebody take them down in the morning," Ratcher said. "And thanks, Ira, for getting here so fast on such short notice."

"I'm glad I could help out. I hope you catch the son-ofabitch who did it."

Chief Ratcher's mouth was set in a grim line. "I hope so too." He turned away from the bodies and walked out of the room. Kirby Franklin followed.

The scientific investigation team from the San Diego County sheriff's office arrived on schedule. They unloaded their cameras and equipment, and began going through the big house, starting in the basement. As he'd promised, Kirby stayed in the background watching them work. When they finished down there and moved on upstairs, Kirby stayed in the rec room staring thoughtfully at the floor.

Chief Ratcher came clumping down the stairs to join him. "They found something in the kitchen."

"Oh?"

"Bloodstains and traces of skin tissue in the sink drain. It looks like that's where the boy was killed."

Kirby gestured down at the figures painted on the floor. "What do you make of all this?"

Ratcher looked down and shrugged his heavy shoulders. "Damned if I know. Probably a game of some kind. Edith was always involved in some crazy thing or other." He looked up at Kirby. "Your friend Mrs. Cross was going around with Edith and her bunch, wasn't she?"

"She saw them once or twice a week."

"It might be worthwhile talking to her. You want to set it up?"

"I'll do what I can," Kirby said.

Ratcher studied him. "Is there something else on your mind?"

"It occurs to me that if Philip Werhaus did freak out for some reason, Diana could be in danger."

"That's a possibility," Ratcher admitted. "I've got men out looking for him, and when the sheriff's people are through here I'll have somebody stake out the house in case he comes back."

"I think I'll go over now and make sure Diana's all right," Kirby said.

"You won't tell her too much?" said Ratcher. "I don't want to start a panic before we have some solid evidence."

"Diana isn't the type to panic," Kirby said. "And considering the possible danger, I think she has a right to know what's happening."

"Fair enough," said the chief. "If she knows anything we don't, you'll put her in touch with me?"

"Will do."

The men from the sheriff's office were just finishing up on the ground floor and starting up the stairs when Kirby left the house. He drove the three miles to Diana's cottage with a growing sense of anxiety.

Diana sat pale but composed on the sofa and listened as Kirby told her about the discovery of the two bodies in the yard behind Edith's house. He left out only the details of how little Timmy Werhaus had been dismembered.

"Do they think Philip did it?" she asked when Kirby had finished.

"When a wife or family members are killed the husband is always the automatic top suspect," he said. "He's been acting suspiciously since last weekend. He hasn't gone into his L.A. office all week. Then there was the business here last night." Kirby stopped talking as he saw that Diana's mind was somewhere else.

"Is there something you're not telling me?" he asked.

"What do you mean?"

"You've been pretty friendly with Edith and her group since you came to town, haven't you?"

"I suppose so. Actually, I'm closer to Harriet Nagle than to the others."

"You were all up at Edith's last Saturday night, weren't you?"

"Yes."

"I was down in the basement recreation room today. There are a lot of queer symbols painted on the floor. I'm no authority on witchcraft, but it looked to me like a layout for some kind of Satanic ritual."

He paused for a moment. Diana said nothing.

"Did that have anything to do with your group?"

Diana drew in a deep breath before she spoke. "I think it all may have more to do with me than with Edith or any of the others."

Kirby sat looking at her, his eyes full of questions.

"Are you ready for a really fantastic story?" Diana said.

"Try me."

Diana looked up at the clock on the mantel. "Matt is supposed to come back up from the beach in an hour. That should give me time to tell you most of it. I guess the place to start is with a day last April when Matt and I went up into the mountains for a picnic...."

During the next hour Diana told Kirby everything she could remember about the circumstances that had brought her to Tranquilo Beach. She told him about the apparition in the fog, the ill-fated séance, and the "demon-raising" session at Edith's house, including Edith's peculiar behavior afterward. She recounted the unexplainable happenings of her childhood, and told of her visits to Dr. Letterman and Saul Julian looking for help.

When she had finished, she leaned back and looked at Kirby. "Now, what's your diagnosis? My shrink thinks I'm crazy and my psychic thinks I'm haunted, or something close to it."

"I don't know what to think," Kirby said. "I mean, séances and demons are not something the editor of a beach-town weekly runs into every day."

Diana's eyes were serious. "Kirby, if you want out now, it's okay. I understand. You and I have enjoyed each other, and I know you've been very good for me. I'll always be glad I came down here because of you. But you didn't agree to take on a lady with demons or ghosts or whatever the hell it is following her around. If you want to walk away now, I won't blame you a bit. And no hard feelings, okay?"

"Are you through?" Kirby said.

"I'm through."

"Then come over here."

He pulled her over next to him on the sofa and kissed her with feeling. Diana's response was stiff for a moment, then she relaxed and let her body mold itself to his. She was breathing hard when at last they broke apart.

"Did you really think I'd bolt for the door at the first sign of a problem?" he said.

"Kirby, this is no ordinary problem."

"I can see that. But whatever it turns out to be— demon, bogeyman, or bill collector—maybe it won't be so big with two of us fighting it."

Diana searched his face, trying to read the expression there. "You don't believe me, do you?"

"Dammit, don't be obstinate. I believe that everything you told me happened just the way you described it. I also happen to believe that there's a natural explanation for all of it. Together we can find out what it is."

"Nothing would make me happier," Diana said with feeling.

"Then let's get on with it," he said. "Where do you want to start?"

She looked at the clock again. "I think I'd like to start by bringing Matt home. I'm a little worried about him."

"That's easy enough," Kirby said. "Let's go get him."

16

Philip Werhaus, or more accurately, the thing that now inhabited Philip's body, crouched among the scrub oaks on the hillside behind the big stone house. Silently he watched the activity below. Men in the uniform of the county sheriff came and went. There was also Bo Ratcher, the fat chief of police, and that meddling bastard Kirby Franklin. They tramped in and out of the house and over the grounds. There was a conspicuous raw hole in the flower bed along the rear wall.

Philip supposed he should have been more careful in disposing of the woman and the child. But how could he have foreseen that those two brats and their mangy dog would come snooping around the house when no one was there and dig up the bodies? Anyway, Philip had expected that by this time his work would be done. It was simply a piece of foul luck, the untimely arrival of Kirby Franklin last night. It was the first good opportunity Philip had found to be alone with Diana Cross. There was not likely to be another. At least not while he was using the present body. Soon the news of the killings would be out, and Philip Werhaus would not be free to show his face anywhere in Tranquilo Beach.

The beast that lived within him now raged in frustration. The tiny part of the mind that still belonged to Philip Werhaus cried out in terrible silent pain.

Another car pulled up in front of the house, and two young men got out. Philip recognized them as coaches from the local high school who filled in during the summer as reserve policemen. Chief Ratcher came out of the house to meet them. They stood for a minute, talking on the sidewalk. Ratcher pointed up at the hillside behind the house.

Philip thought for a moment that he had been seen, but he soon realized the policemen were talking too casually for that. From their attitudes and gestures, he deduced that Ratcher was telling the two young men to hide up on the hillside and wait for him to come home so they could capture him. Fools. Did they think it was going to be that easy?

Kirby Franklin came out of the house then and said something to the chief as though he were leaving. They talked for a minute, then Kirby crossed the street and got into his old top-down Mustang.

Carrying the news to Diana Cross, Philip assumed. If there were time, he would have much enjoyed making the nosy newspaperman suffer, but far more important was Diana Cross. She was, after all, the sole reason for the presence of the demon Astragoth on earth. It would now be impossible to approach her as Philip Werhaus, but there were other ways.

Staying concealed in the heavy chaparral, Philip worked his way along the hillside parallel to the road until he was well away from the house and out of sight. Far behind him he could see the two young policemen laboriously climbing up the slope. They would have a long wait. He dropped down to the road and began to move swiftly along the shoulder toward the town.

The child, he decided, was the key. Philip had met Matthew once when Diana brought him along to pick

124

up Edith. He seemed to be an open and friendly little boy. He would most likely be on the beach now, and he would still have no reason to fear Philip Werhaus. He quickened his pace, heading for the ocean.

Nancy Urich pulled off her shoes and carried them as she crossed the sand toward the lifeguard tower. She paused halfway there to look at her brother. Guy sat like the king of the beach—tall, blond, toasted to a shade of golden brown that was the envy of tourists and beach people alike. He wore tight red trunks and dark-tinted glasses, tirelessly scanning the water and the shoreline, watching over his subjects.

As usual, a cluster of lithe young girls had their towels spread out around the foot of the tower. They peeled away as much of their swim suits as the beach rules allowed, talked brightly among themselves, and vied for the attentions of the handsome lifeguard. Nancy could not blame them. Had he not been her brother, she could have gone for Guy herself. Even though, she hastened to add mentally, he could at times be an awful pill.

A group of children were playing happily at the water's edge under the watchful eye of her brother. Nancy knew all of them, having been baby-sitter for most. They waved to her and she waved back.

One of the children ran up the sand to meet her. She waved to little Matthew Cross.

"Hi, Nancy," he said, giving her a wide smile.

"Hi, Matt. How's the water?"

"Good. Really warm. Are you coming in?"

"Not today."

"Why not?"

"Haven't got time."

"Will you sometime, though? I'm a good swimmer. I could keep up with you, I bet."

"I bet you could," she said. "One of these days we'll try it, Matt."

She watched the little boy run back to join the others, and smiled with affection. It pleased her to know that the children liked her and trusted her. Taking care of them was a joy for Nancy. She recognized the special world that children live in, and they accepted her into it. She planned to have at least four of her own. She was confident that she would be a good mother.

She reached the foot of the wooden lifeguard tower and ignored the cool glances of the other girls there to reach up and tweak her brother's big toe.

He looked down and grinned at her. "Hey, Squirrely, what's happening?"

"I need to borrow your car, sex god."

"No way."

"No, seriously, Mom needs some things from the store and she's got a dead battery."

"Why doesn't she wait until Dad gets home and use his?"

"Because she needs the stuff for dinner, and that'll be too late. Come on, Scrooge, be nice. I won't put any dents in your pussy wagon."

Guy looked around quickly to see if anyone had heard. "You know I don't like to hear you talk that way."

Nancy gave him her sweetest smile. "I know, I only do it to shake you up."

"You think that's smart when you're trying to borrow my car?"

"Please, Guy, I'll have it back here in half an hour."

"Oh, all right." Guy opened the wooden box under his chair and fished through the suntan oil and first-aid equipment for his car keys. When he found them he held them for a moment just out of Nancy's reach.

"When I get off today I am going over every inch of

that car with a magnifying glass. Every inch. If I find even the tiniest scratch..."

"I will drive the thing like it's made out of glass," Nancy said. "Gimme the keys."

Guy dropped them into her open hand.

"Thanks, sex god." She made an exaggerated kissing mouth at him and swung off down the beach, her slim golden legs flashing in the sun.

Not a bad-looking kid for only sixteen, Guy thought. Two or three more years and she would be a real beauty. He hoped she would find the right kind of a guy.

His attention was attracted by a man wearing a business suit, standing at the edge of the sand. Nobody came down to the beach wearing a suit. Guy looked more closely and saw it was Philip Werhaus from the big house down on the cliff. He was on the point of walking over to see if there was some problem, when Mr. Werhaus turned away and was lost from sight among the cars in the parking lot.

Guy turned back to check the beach in the other direction and saw Diana Cross and Kirby Franklin coming toward him. He waved at them, then leaned forward toward the children playing in the surf.

"Hey, Matt," he called, "what time were you supposed to be home?"

"No special time," Matt said, looking guilty.

"Well, if you're late, you'd better have an excuse ready, because here comes your mom."

Matt brushed the sand from his knees and walked across the sand toward his mother and Kirby Franklin. When he saw they were smiling, he relaxed.

"Is it time to go already?" he asked.

"It is for today," Diana told him.

"Nobody else has to go this early."

"Your mother and I are going out for hamburgers,"

Kirby told him. "If you don't want to go along, I suppose we could leave you here."

"Can I have a quarter-pounder?"

"With cheese, if you want it."

"I'll be right back," said Matt. He scampered back across the beach to get his towel.

"What's all this about hamburgers?" Diana said. "I thought we were going to the dinner theater tonight."

"That's not till later," Kirby said. He pointed at Matt hurrying back to join them. "It's better than a long argument about whether it's too early to come home, isn't it?"

Diana punched him lightly on the arm. "My master psychologist."

Matt ran back, spraying wet sand, to join them. "I'm all ready," he said. "Can I have a bag of fries too?"

"Ask the big spender here," Diana told him.

"The sky's the limit, my boy," Kirby said grandly. "The sky's the limit."

From back among the cars in the beach parking lot Philip Werhaus watched the three of them walk off up the beach. If only he had been here five minutes earlier, he could have lured the boy away. The lips peeled back from his teeth in a mask of demonic rage. At the sound of approaching footsteps his face returned to the normal bland expression of Philip Werhaus.

Nancy Urich was running over in her mind the list of things she was to pick up for her mother as she walked between the angle-parked cars in the beach lot. She started violently when a man stepped out from between two cars directly into her path.

"Oh, Nancy, I'm sorry," he said, "I didn't mean to frighten you."

"Oh, hi, Mr. Werhaus. You just surprised me. I was thinking about something else."

He looked down at the car keys in her hand. "Are you driving into town, by any chance?"

"Well...I have to go to the market and pick up some things for my mother."

"I need to get to the bank before it closes," Philip said. "I'd sure appreciate a lift."

Nancy tried to think of a graceful way to refuse. Guy would have an absolute fit if he thought she was giving anybody—*anybody*—a ride in his precious car. But how could he object to Mr. Werhaus? He was always pleasant and nice to everybody. A quiet man, timid almost, but surely nice enough.

She looked at him more closely as he stood smiling, waiting for her answer. He seemed different somehow. His eyes seemed to draw her to him. There was an odd red tinge to them, not like bloodshot, but like a smoldering fire. She had never noticed before, but he was really quite handsome, for an older man. Right now, in fact, he looked a little bit like Clint Eastwood.

Suddenly Nancy realized she had been staring. She pulled her eyes away.

"If it's out of your way, don't worry about it," Philip said. "I can probably make it at a fast walk."

"No, it's all right. I'll be glad to drop you off." Nancy felt all warm and soft, and did not know why. What she did know was that she liked the feeling. "I'm using my brother's car. It's right over there."

They walked together to the gleaming cherry-lacquered Trans-Am. Nancy got in behind the wheel and leaned across the seat to pop the door lock on the passenger's side.

Philip got in and settled beside her in the soft acrylic fur of the bucket seat. "This is really a treat for me," he said. "I hope some of my friends see me being chauffeured through town by a beautiful young woman."

He spoke slowly, his voice soft in a way that made Nancy tingle. She had been told by boys before that she was pretty, but this was not a boy, this was a man. And he had called her a *woman*.

There was a musky smell inside the car that Nancy thought must be Philip's shaving lotion. She caught herself breathing too rapidly. Foolishly, she could not take her eyes off the man. He smiled and leaned toward her. She felt the heat of his hand as he touched her face. Then before she knew what was happening, he was kissing her. A part of Nancy seemed to stand aside and look on in dismay at what was happening to her, but the rest of her returned the kiss with eager, openmouthed abandon.

He said, "Let's go somewhere."

Her mind screamed, *No, no, let me alone!*

But her body murmured, "Yes!"

17

"Are you going to marry Kirby?" Matthew asked.

Diana was at the kitchen counter preparing a plate of cookies for Nancy Urich tonight when she came to sit with Matt. She stopped and thought for a moment about Matt's question. Then she turned to look down into the grave little face of her son.

"Kirby hasn't asked me to marry him," she said.

"I know, but what if he does?"

Diana turned away from the counter. "Let's go into the living room and talk about it."

They walked out through the archway into the living room and Diana sat down on the sofa. Matthew, being very adult, took the chair facing her.

"How do you feel about Kirby and me?" she asked.

Matt shrugged. "Oh, okay, I guess."

"How would you feel about him being your father?"

"But what about Daddy?"

"You would still have him, Matt. He'll always be your real father. But if I should marry Kirby, or some-one else, he would be your stepfather. Then you'd have two."

"Kirby or *who* else?" the boy asked suspiciously.

Diana smiled. "I was just playing what-if. Right now the only one we're talking about is Kirby."

"He'd be okay, I guess," Matt said. "He likes to do things that are fun, and he doesn't treat me like a little kid."

"Then you like him?"

"Sure. He doesn't get mad all the time."

"Well, not often," Diana agreed. "But remember, this is all just *maybe* talk. I told you he hasn't asked me to marry him."

"He probably will."

"Do you think so?"

"He looks like he's going to."

"It's possible."

"Will you if he does? Marry him?"

"That's something I'd have to think about long and hard. If he does ask me, you and I will talk it over again before I make any decision. Okay?"

"Okay." Matt bounced out of the chair and became a five-year-old again. "Can I have a cookie?"

"May I."

"May I have a cookie?"

"Just one. I don't want you to spoil your appetite for dinner. If you behave, maybe Nancy will let you have another one with milk before bedtime."

"I always behave," Matthew said.

"Sure you do."

"Can I have my cookie now?"

"Help yourself."

Matt dashed off into the kitchen and came back with his mouth full of chocolate-chip cookie. "Thanks, Mom," he said.

"You're welcome."

The doorbell rang and Diana walked over to answer it. Nancy Urich stood outside.

"Hi, Nancy, come on in. It will be a few minutes before I'm ready to leave."

"That's all right, Diana, take your time. I'll just make myself comfortable."

Diana turned and looked more closely at the girl. She had never before called Diana by her first name. Nancy smiled at her, but tonight the smile seemed to be a touch brighter than usual.

"I made some cookies," Diana said, continuing to watch the girl. "They're out in the kitchen for you to help yourself. After dinner, if Matt's been good, you can give him one with milk before bedtime."

Nancy smiled and nodded, but Diana had the odd feeling that the girl hadn't heard a word she'd said.

"That's an awfully pretty dress, Diana," Nancy said. She came close and reached out to stroke the material.

Reflexively Diana edged away from the girl's touch. "It's just an old summertime thing," she said.

"It really shows off your figure. You do have a terrific figure, Diana."

"Uh, thank you." For some reason she could not name, Diana felt terribly uncomfortable with the girl. She looked around, at a loss for something to say.

"You didn't bring a book tonight?" she asked finally.

"Books are boring. There are lots better ways to pass the time. Don't you think so?"

"I suppose," Diana said, feeling increasingly nervous. "You know you can use the television any time you want to."

Matt came dashing back into the room. "Hi, Nancy. Mom said I could have cookies after dinner."

"I already told her about that," Diana said.

Matt came to a sudden stop and was looking at Nancy.

"How's my big boy?" she said, and walked across the room to him. She bent her knees to bring her face to a level with his. She put a hand on the boy's shoulder and moved it around to massage the back of his neck. "Have you got a kiss for Nancy?"

Matthew looked down at the floor, grinning in embarrassment.

"The cookies are out in the kitchen," Diana said. "Why don't you go out and get them, Matt?" She heard herself talking louder than necessary.

The boy pulled himself free of Nancy's embrace and went out of the room. Nancy walked back to the sofa and sat down. Diana could not take her eyes off the girl. Her movements were slow and graceful, not the energetic dashing about of a sixteen-year-old girl. She smiled up at Diana. Somehow, the smile was out of place, a little off-center.

"Nancy, is there anything wrong tonight?"

The girl's eyes went wide and innocent. And yet, not quite innocent. "Wrong? I don't know what you mean."

"You just seem, well, different."

"I can't imagine why. I feel just the same as I always do."

Matthew came back into the room carrying the plate of cookies. He looked hopefully at Diana. She gave him a quick shake of her head.

Nancy took the plate of cookies from him and set it down on the coffee table. "Come on up here and sit in my lap," she said.

Matt shrugged his narrow shoulders and shifted embarrassedly from foot to foot.

"Come on," Nancy coaxed. "You and I are old friends now. There's no need to be shy with old friends. Aren't you my boyfriend?"

"Aww." Matthew was blushing furiously, but obviously enjoying the attention.

Nancy reached out and grasped him under the arms. With surprising ease she hoisted him off the floor and set him down in her lap.

134

"There now, that's not such a bad place to sit, is it?" she said.

She tickled Matt's ribs, and he laughed.

"Pretty soon it will be the other way around. You'll be having the girls sit in your lap." She gave him an enthusiastic hug. "Do you know that?"

"Not me," Matt said, grinning.

"Oh yes you will. You're going to set the girls right down on your lap." She patted the tops of his thighs. "Right there. And you're going to like it when they do."

Diana suddenly found her voice. "I think Matt's getting too big to be sitting in laps."

"No he isn't. He's just the right size. And he likes it too." She slid her hand along the boy's lean flanks. "Don't you like it, Matthew?"

"Nancy—" Diana began, but broke off at the sound of the doorbell. She hurried to answer it and was relieved to see Kirby had arrived.

"Kirby, I'm so glad you're here," she said with feeling. "Come in. Please come in."

He looked at her curiously for a moment. "Well, I'm glad to see you too." He stepped into the living room. "Hi, Matt. How's it going, Nancy?"

Matthew squirmed out of the girl's lap and dashed over to Kirby for their ritual of measuring his height. The top of Matt's head came just to Kirby's pockets.

"Will you look at that!" Kirby exclaimed. "I think you've grown another inch."

"Really?"

"Well, almost."

"Am I gonna be as big as you someday, Kirby?"

"Bigger, most likely."

"Wow!"

Nancy rose gracefully from the sofa and walked over to join them. Diana watched, shocked at the new seductive roll of the girl's hips.

"Hello, Mr. Franklin," Nancy said, standing close and looking up at him.

Diana noted that although she still appended the "mister" to his name, she gave it an oddly provocative inflection.

Kirby cocked his head and looked down at the girl in a speculative way. "Are you doing something different with your hair?"

She gave him the bright, slightly lopsided smile. "It's just the same old hair. All I did was brush it forward a little bit in front."

"Well, whatever it is, you're looking exceptionally pretty tonight."

Nancy lowered her eyes, but only for a moment, then she was gazing back up at Kirby. "Why, thank you, Mr. Franklin."

"Oh, Kirby," Diana said. She spoke loudly to interrupt the strange communication she saw developing between the man and the girl.

He turned, reluctantly, Diana thought, to include her in the company. "Yes?"

"Would it be all right with you if we had dinner here tonight instead of going out?"

"But I got reservations at the dinner theater for *Chapter Two.* The show closes tomorrow, so this will be our last chance to see it."

"I know, but I'm just feeling kind of tired tonight. There are steaks in the freezer. It wouldn't take any time at all to thaw them out."

"I don't get it," Kirby said. "You told me you were crazy about Neil Simon."

"It's really a good show," Nancy put in. "I saw the movie."

"Good for you," Diana said sharply. "Look, I just don't feel like going out tonight. Do I have to get everyone's approval to stay home?"

136

Matt stood across the room watching with large eyes as the grown-ups talked in loud voices.

Nancy remained calm. "You don't have to worry about anything here. I'll take good care of Matt."

"I don't want to discuss it." Diana snatched up her purse from the coffee table and dug into it for her wallet. "Here, I'll pay you for tonight anyway. I just don't feel like going out."

"Oh, I couldn't take the money for not doing anything," Nancy said.

"Yes you can," Diana insisted. She peeled several bills out of the wallet and thrust them at the girl. "Here. Take it."

Kirby moved forward. "Diana, what's the matter with you?"

She whirled to face him. "Nothing is the matter with me. I changed my mind about going out, that's all. I'd rather stay here and cook steaks and have a relaxing evening. Does that mean there's something the matter with me?"

"No, Diana," he said in a measured tone. "You're free to change your mind as many times as you want to."

"I guess I'd better go," Nancy said. Her eyes were bright as she watched the two of them.

"Can I give you a ride home?" Kirby asked.

Nancy moved a step closer to him. "I'd like that. If it's no trouble, I mean."

"It's no trouble," Kirby said.

Diana spoke up quickly. "Kirby, don't go."

He looked at her in surprise. "It will just take me five minutes."

"I want you to stay with me now. Please."

Kirby gave her a long look, then turned back to the girl. "If you don't mind, Nancy..."

"Sure, that's all right," she said. "I can walk home easy enough."

As the girl went out the door her eyes caught and held Diana's for just a moment. Diana thought she recognized something there, but the door closed between them.

"All right," Kirby said when they were alone, "do you want to tell me what this is all about?"

"Just a minute." She turned to Matthew, who was watching the whole scene, fascinated. "Why don't you run along to your room and play?"

"I don't want to play in my room."

"Matthew!" she said with a rising inflection.

"Can I have some cookies?"

"Take them with you."

"And the TV?"

"Yes, yes, anything." She strode across the room and unplugged the portable television set. She rolled the stand down the hall and into Matthew's bedroom and plugged it in again. "Now don't play it too loud, understand?"

Matt was already working the channel selector, eating a cookie from his free hand. "I won't."

Diana paused outside his door to light a cigarette and take a deep, calming drag. Then she walked back to the living room. Kirby was standing there stiffly, waiting for her.

"I know I'm not making a lot of sense," she said, "but please bear with me."

"This isn't a replay of last Sunday night, is it?" Kirby said.

"No. I acted childishly then, but this time it's different. I'm afraid, Kirby."

"Afraid? Of what?"

"I can't tell you exactly. I just know I don't want to

leave Matt with Nancy." When the words were out, Diana realized how silly they must sound.

"You've been leaving Matt with her for more than a month," he reminded her.

"I know, but tonight she was...different. Didn't you see it?"

Kirby frowned thoughtfully. "I guess she was a little livelier than usual. That doesn't seem like anything to get excited about."

"I tell you, Kirby, there is something wrong about Nancy Urich tonight." Diana paced the room as she talked, trying to put her thoughts in order. She badly wanted Kirby on her side, and she felt she was losing him. "I know it sounds crazy, but I had the same feeling about her tonight that I had about Philip Werhaus when he came here." As she said it, Diana was struck with how much the girl's actions reminded her of the way Edith had come on that last night at the big house on the cliff.

"Diana, that doesn't make any sense at all," Kirby said.

"I told you it sounded crazy." She came back and put her arms around him, resting her cheek against his chest. "Can you indulge me until I get some things straight in my head? Just stay with me tonight and be nice to me. How about it?"

He gave her a hug that brought the air out of her lungs with a little squeak. "Okay," he said, "no more questions tonight. But sooner or later I'm going to want some kind of an explanation."

"You'll get it, I promise you," she said. "You know, Kirby Franklin, you are a heck of a guy."

"I know," he said, nuzzling her hair.

She stepped back self-consciously and smoothed her dress. "I'd better go start doing things with those steaks."

"Good idea," he said. "I'll go get Matt and the TV set and bring them back out here. And see if there are any cookies left."

Diana pulled his head down and kissed him. "You know, mister, I think I love you."

"You really *are* in a peculiar mood tonight," he said, but his smile told her all she wanted to know.

Kirby went out to get Matt, and something made Diana shiver. Before she started for the kitchen, she checked the front door to be sure it was locked.

18

The thing that now lived in the body of Nancy Urich
raged silently as Nancy walked away from the cottage.
It was clear that Diana Cross was beginning to sense
too much. She should have been more careful, Nancy
thought; or so thought the thing that was now using
Nancy's brain. She had been overconfident that Diana
would let down her guard against the nice little baby-
sitter. But something had given her away. It was another failure. Just as Edith Werhaus and then her husband, Philip, had failed with Diana, now Nancy Urich
had failed.

Instead of going directly home, where she would
have to explain why she was back early from the sitting
job, Nancy walked down to the dark, deserted beach.
There she sat and gazed out over the water while the
last glimmer of the sunset faded and the stars blinked
on one by one overhead.

One valuable piece of knowledge had come out of
tonight's failure. Diana Cross had a weakness. A serious one. She might be on guard now against anyone
who acted strangely, but she was still intensely vulnerable through the little boy. Matthew was the key
to Diana Cross.

Tonight it would have been so easy to take the boy,

141

had the mother not sensed the danger. However, there would be other chances, new directions to come from. And it was the threat of danger to the boy that was important, that would finally defeat Diana.

Nancy Urich stood up and brushed the sand off her jeans. She left the beach and walked up the hill toward the comfortable white house where her parents lived.

Earl and Irene Urich were secure in the belief that they had found the best of all possible worlds. It had been quite different ten years ago. Then Earl, a design engineer, was laid off in one of the recurring upheavals of the aerospace industry in Los Angeles. At the age of thirty-six he was without a job, without prospects, and with a wife and two children aged six and eight to support.

Like many others at the time, he enrolled in real estate school. While most of the others dropped out, Earl stuck with it and obtained his license.

Irene went back to work as secretary to an accountant and helped pay the bills during the next couple of years. Earl hung in there during the tedious period of knocking on doors, looking for listings. To his own surprise, he found that he had a natural affinity for the business. People liked him, and that was half the battle.

Within three years he had his own brokerage and a staff of eager young agents working for him. In another year he was able to move his family out of smoggy Los Angeles and into the comfortable house in Tranquilo Beach.

The children had turned out as well as any parents could hope for. Guy was an A student, a handsome and popular boy, and next year he started on full scholarship at Stanford. Nancy was pretty and bright, and had never given them five minutes of worry. In a time of rebellious, dope-using, sex-obsessed teenagers, the Urich kids shaped up pretty damn well. So thought the parents.

When Nancy had returned this afternoon more than an hour overdue from a trip to the market, it was so unlike her that her mother thought there must be something wrong with the girl. Nancy had assured her it was nothing. Just a slow checkout line at the market.

Still, Irene Urich had continued to watch her daughter throughout the afternoon. There was something vaguely different about her. A certain flush to her cheeks, a brightness of her eyes. When Nancy left to sit for the evening with little Matthew Cross, Irene had mentioned it to her husband.

"Just normal high spirits," was Earl's diagnosis. "Teenage girls have to act up a little now and then. I'll bet you did when you were her age."

"I suppose so," Irene had agreed, but she could not rid herself of the uneasy feeling that there was something wrong with her daughter.

When Nancy returned home from the baby-sitting job it was a few minutes before midnight. As usual, her parents had waited up for her, while trying to appear to be doing no such thing. Her father sat reading a new John Le Carré spy novel while her mother watched an old Joan Crawford movie on television with the volume turned way down.

Earl looked up and smiled as his daughter came in. "Hi, Nance. How'd it go?"

"No problems." The girl's eyes ranged around the living room. "Where's Guy?"

"He went up to bed about an hour ago," Irene said. "He went out after dinner and played volleyball for a couple of hours. Came home exhausted."

"Serves him right," Nancy said and started for the stairs.

"Just a minute, dear," Irene said.

Nancy hesitated and half turned toward her mother. "Are you sure you're feeling all right?"

"I'm fine," Nancy said quickly. "Great. Why?"

Irene studied her daughter's face. Again she felt the undefinable strangeness of the girl. "I don't know. Your eyes look funny. I do hope you're not coming down with something."

Nancy looked away. "No, really, I'm okay. I was reading under a lamp that wasn't bright enough, that's all."

"You ought to be more careful," her father said. "We only get one pair of eyes, you know."

"I'll be careful," Nancy said. She turned away and walked out of the room.

Earl and Irene Urich looked at each other.

"Do you think I ought to go up and talk to her?" Irene asked.

"She says she's all right."

"I know, but she's acting kind of funny. Didn't you see it?"

"She does seem to be a bit off her feed today. Maybe she's got a new boyfriend."

"I hope that's all it is."

"If you're still worried about her in the morning, have Frank Kincaid take a look at her."

"I'm probably worried about nothing," Irene said.

"You wouldn't be a mother if you weren't," Earl said fondly.

Earl marked his place in the book and put it away, Irene turned off the television set, and they went back to their bedroom.

Upstairs Nancy slipped into her own room and closed the door. She stood for a moment with her ear against it, listening. The beast that lived within her was restive. The latest failure was still a bitter memory. The

144

beast would not let this night go by without taking some kind of action.

After ten minutes Nancy opened her bedroom door again. She stood holding her breath in the dark hallway and listening for sounds in the house. Downstairs the television set was off, and there was a faint rustle of movement from the back bedroom where her parents slept. And from Guy's room, two doors down the hall, came the sound of her brother's slow, regular breathing.

Nancy closed the door to her room silently behind her. Barefoot, she padded down the hall to her brother's door. She grasped the knob and turned it slowly so it would make no sound. She pushed the door open just far enough for her to step inside, then closed it again.

Nancy had no trouble seeing in the dark through the eyes of the creature that had taken her body. Guy lay on his back, sleeping naked as he always did, with only a sheet to cover him. The deep tan of his chest and shoulders was stark against the white sheets. Silently Nancy moved closer to the bed.

Her brother's body was clearly outlined beneath the sheet. His chest had broadened in the last year, but the ribs were still visible. His stomach was flat and hard. His long legs had the smooth, well-defined muscles of the swimmer. And between his legs...

Nancy leaned closer to look at her brother's penis outlined beneath the sheet. Even flaccid as it was now in sleep, it had a good length and thickness. She smiled, a curious combination of innocence and depravity.

She had seen her brother naked before, of course, when by accident she met him on his way to or from the shower. But it had never been more than a glimpse, as Guy always grabbed for something to cover himself and Nancy turned away embarrassed. Now, although it was the beast that was controlling her, the tiny portion of Nancy's own mind that still functioned wanted to look at her brother's body. See what he had down there. Touch it.

Very gently she peeled the sheet down to the foot of the bed. She stood looking down at her naked sleeping brother, savoring the moment. Then she stripped off her own clothes and lay down beside him.

In his sleep Guy felt the naked female body next to him and had an immediate erection. In his dream it was the body of Marcie Quinn. She was a dark-haired, flirty-eyed girl who had transferred to the T-Beach high school from Portland halfway through last semester. Guy had dated her several times. There had been some steamy sessions on a blanket spread over the sand, but they had never gone all the way. Marcie had gone back up north with her parents on vacation; Guy lived with fantasies of her soft, supple body, and what they would do to each other if ever they got the chance.

Now in his dream he felt Marcie's hands moving expertly over his body, squeezing, caressing. Now she was kissing his naked flesh in a way he hadn't even imagined. My God, was she going to...? Yes! She had taken his cock in her mouth. Oh, Jesus!

Guy awoke with a start to see that he was not dreaming at all. The sheet that had covered him was gone. And there kneeling over him with her plump little lips on his penis was his sister.

"Jesus Christ, Nancy, what are you doing?"

She let his cock slide slowly out of her mouth, giving the purpled head a little flick with her tongue as it came free.

Nancy looked at him with wide, mocking eyes. "I'm sucking you off, darling brother. What does it look like I'm doing?"

Maddeningly, his erection would not go down. He sat up and made a grab for the sheet. Nancy seized his shoulder and with more strength than a girl should have she pushed him back down on the mattress.

"You're not going to tell me you didn't like it," she said.

"Have you gone crazy?" Guy's voice cracked, and he cleared his throat self-consciously.

"You don't really want me to stop, do you?"

"For God's sake, Nancy, you're my *sister!*"

"What difference does that make? If it feels good, do it. Isn't that the way it goes?" She took hold of his penis again and bent over him suddenly, taking the head into her mouth like a lollipop. She looked up into his eyes while her teeth and tongue did wild things to him down below.

"It's wrong," he said, but his protest was only a whisper now.

Nancy rode up and down on his shaft while Guy rolled his head on the pillow and moaned. She let her lips slide off again with a wet little pop, and crawled higher on the bed to look into her brother's face.

"Did you ever wonder what you taste like down there?" Her voice was husky, almost a growl. "I've got your taste in my mouth now. Do you want to try it?"

Nancy's mouth came down on his, and for a moment Guy kept his lips tight together. But only for a moment, then he yielded. His sister's tongue slid past his lips, between his teeth, and deep into his head. He tasted, as she had promised, the slightly medicinal tang of his own juices.

After that Guy Urich struggled no more. He put his hands on his sister's shoulders and rolled her over onto her back. He took his position between her legs. Nancy smiled up at him in her new mocking way and drew her knees up. She offered him her cunt, and he took it.

The explosion of passion was like nothing he had ever known. And then came the pain.

19

The morning sun was warm and bright. It made a cheerful crosshatch pattern on the wall across from the window in Chief Bo Ratcher's office in the Tranquilo Beach City Hall. In a cypress tree just outside the window a mockingbird ran through its repertoire of tweets and warbles.

The faces of the three men in the room were a grim contrast to the cheerful morning. Chief Ratcher, Kirby Franklin, and pathologist Ira Sussman spoke in dull monotones as they examined a sheaf of blown-up glossy photographs of dead people.

"Now Philip Werhaus too," the chief said. "Jesus, that makes a whole family wiped out."

"You say they found him last night?" Kirby asked.

"That's right," the chief said. "The body was in a clump of oleander just off the shoulder of Bayview Road. What it looks like is somebody threw the body out of a car."

Kirby turned to the pathologist. "What killed him?"

"I wish I could tell you," said Sussman.

"I wish you could too," Chief Ratcher said with feeling.

"Any guesses?" Kirby persisted.

"I don't guess," the pathologist said primly. "All I

can tell you is that there was no sign of external injury, but inside he's all torn up."

"Just like his wife," Ratcher commented.

"Just like the wife."

"What was the final verdict on the cause of Edith's death?" Kirby asked.

Sussman gave a snort of mirthless laughter. "Death from unknown causes."

"Big help," said Ratcher, mopping a sheen of perspiration from his forehead.

"Could it be some kind of a disease?" Kirby asked.

"No disease I ever heard of does that to a person's insides," said Sussman. "Not without they've been sick for a very long time. And that is apparently not the case with these people."

"No," Ratcher confirmed, "both of them were reported to be up and around and healthy shortly before their deaths."

"And then there is the business with the brains," Sussman continued. "They look like they had battery acid poured over them."

"What about poison?" Kirby suggested.

"If it is a poison, it is a new one to me, and the most horrible since phosgene gas."

"But it *is* possible?"

"Sure, it's possible," the pathologist admitted.

Kirby scribbled in a small notebook. Chief Ratcher watched him nervously.

"You're not going to write this up for the *Tide,* are you, Kirby?" said Ratcher.

"How could I *not* print it, Bo? All three members of one of our best-known families are mysteriously dead. The little boy brutally murdered, and the parents dead from some 'unknown cause' that ravaged their insides and ate away their brains. There's no way I could ignore a story like that."

"But think of the terrible publicity it will be for the town."

"The *Tide* is supposed to be a newspaper, Bo, not a Chamber of Commerce handout. Anyway, the metropolitan dailies are sure to get hold of the story. There's no way we can cover it up."

"I'm not talking cover-up," the chief said hastily. "What I mean is play it down. No big scare headlines. It won't do anybody any good to make a big sensational thing out of this. What it looks like now is that Philip Werhaus went out of his head and killed his wife and the boy. Now he's dead too, and the whole thing can fade away if we don't make too much of it."

"Excuse me for bringing it up, chief," Sussman said, "but you are overlooking a few important points. In what manner did Philip Werhaus kill his wife that ripped her up inside without leaving external marks? Who or what killed him in the same way? Who dumped his body at the side of the road?"

The chief pushed the photographs of mangled viscera around on his desk and shook his head sadly. "Questions. Jesus, Ira, I've got enough questions. You're supposed to be giving me answers."

There was an uncomfortable silence in the office as the three men avoided each other's eyes. Outside the mockingbird continued his recital.

There was a brisk rap on the door, and a young woman stuck her head into the office.

"Excuse me, chief, there's a call on line one."

"I don't want to talk to anybody until we're through here."

"I know, chief, but this sounds important."

"All right," Ratcher said wearily, and sat down at his desk.

The young woman withdrew her head and closed the door.

The police chief picked up the phone and punched one of the buttons on its base. "Ratcher," he said, and paused to listen. "Hello, doc, what's on your mind?"

As the other two men watched, Chief Ratcher's expression changed from polite interest to concern to anguish. By the time he hung up the telephone he was perspiring freely.

"That was Frank Kincaid," he said. For Sussman's benefit he added, "Frank's a G.P. here in town."

"What's the problem?" Kirby asked.

"He was calling from Earl and Irene Urich's place. Nancy's dead."

Kirby took a step toward him. "Nancy? When did it happen? How?"

"Sometime during the night. The mother said she didn't look just right last night, then this morning she didn't get up for breakfast. Irene went up to the girl's room, found her in bed, not breathing. Earl had left for work and the girl's brother was gone to the beach, so Irene called Frank."

"I just saw Nancy last night," Kirby said. "What did she die of?"

"That's the part I really hate," said Ratcher. He loosened his collar and wiped his neck. "There were no marks of any kind on her." He turned toward the window as though he had just noticed the mockingbird. "Frank Kincaid says there are signs of internal damage. He doesn't know how it could have happened."

"Shit, another one," Sussman said.

"Is it an epidemic of some kind?" Ratcher said.

"An epidemic that dumps bodies out of cars and chops up little boys?"

"Sonofabitch." Ratcher buttoned his collar and pulled

152

the necktie tight again. "We'd better get out there. Are you coming, Kirby?"

The newsman was already moving for the door. "There's somebody I've got to see first. I'll check with you later."

20

Diana got up that morning determined to return to a normal schedule and get some work done. She dressed in an old pair of jeans she had cut off at mid-calf and a man's white shirt, size extra-large, that she liked to wear as a painting smock. She made a big breakfast for herself and Matt, then retired to the room she used for a studio.

The rest of the morning she stood in front of her easel going through the motions. Her hands performed all the familiar tasks—dipping brushes into pots of acrylic color, applying the paint to the posterboard, wiping the brushes, and dipping again. Her mind, however, was far away.

Diana was concerned about her mental state. She had begun to wonder if she was imagining things as Dr. Letterman had suggested. Was she, in fact, becoming a little paranoid? Examining the events of the previous night, she tried to recall just what it was about Nancy Urich's behavior that had upset her so badly. In the clear light of morning, it did not seem nearly as serious as it had the night before.

The whole incident could be explained away as a teenage girl simply being dramatic for one reason or another. What the hell, Diana told herself, Nancy was only sixteen. Girls that age were prone to all sorts of peculiar behavior. Now Diana wondered seriously if she had overreacted. By doing so she might have cost herself the services of a reliable baby-sitter.

That was the way Kirby saw the whole affair. He had stayed with Diana last night, and he had been loving and supportive. However, it was clear that he thought she was being slightly hysterical.

Okay, say for the moment that she had read things into Nancy's behavior. What about Philip Werhaus's coming on to her the other night? She damn sure had not imagined his hand on her leg. And what about Edith? There was no mistaking the fact that she had made a lesbian advance toward Diana that Saturday night after the rec-room session. If the Werhauses were a couple of kinks, they had kept it secret in a small town for a long time.

And if it were only that, the sexual advances, it would be little enough to worry about. Diana had handled propositions before, from both men and women. But there was more here, much more. Something terribly corrupt lurked just under the surface with both Edith and Philip. There was the same sense of depravity in the way Nancy Urich had behaved last night. No, Diana decided, that could not be passed off as play-acting by an imaginative girl. There was a malignancy there, as there had been with Edith and Philip.

Diana worked on. The brushes dipped in and out of the little paint pots, the acrylic colors spread over the posterboard, but the picture taking shape there did not register on Diana's consciousness. Her concentration was given entirely to her other problems.

The sound of a soft footfall behind her made her jump. She whirled from the easel to see Matthew standing in the doorway. He wore an exaggerated expression of boredom.

"Matt, I've asked you not to interrupt me when I'm working," she said.

"I don't have anything to do."

"There's lots to do. Be creative, for heaven's sake."

"I don't want to be creative. I want to go to the beach."

"No. I told you I want you to stay in the house today. Why don't you watch television?"

"There's nothing on but soap operas and those dumb game shows."

"Then play with your toys."

"We left all my best toys back home."

"Well, dammit, can't you find some way to amuse yourself for even a couple of hours? I have other things to do with my time, you know, than finding ways to entertain you!"

Matt's eyes widened suddenly, as though he had been struck in the face. He turned away from her and started out the door.

As soon as the words were out of her mouth Diana regretted them. She dropped the brush she was holding and ran after him.

She knelt on the floor and turned the boy around to face her. "I'm sorry, darling. You haven't done anything wrong, and there is no excuse for me shouting at you. Other things are bothering me, but they're no fault of yours. So I'm sorry. Forgive me?"

Matthew swallowed hard and tried to look manly. "Oh, sure, that's okay. I knew you didn't mean it."

Diana gave him a squeeze and inhaled the fresh summer scent of his fine blond hair. She wanted to tell this small person how much she loved him, how vitally important he was to her world. But that kind of gush would just embarrass him. Anyway, Matt was a bright child. He knew how much he was loved.

"Do you still want to go to the beach?" she said.

A sudden smile lit up his face. "You mean it?"

"I mean it."

"I'll go put on my suit."

Diana caught him by the shirttail as he dashed through the door. "Not so fast, mister."

He turned back suspiciously.

"When you get down to the beach I want you, first thing, to tell Guy you're there."

"He always knows who's there."

"This time I want you to be very sure. And I want you to stay close to Guy's tower where he can see you all the time. Got it?"

"Aww, Mom."

"I'm serious, Matt. Of course, if you'd rather, you can stay home and watch game shows."

"I'll stay close to the tower," Matt said. "Can I go now?"

"In a minute. When you talk to Guy, have him tell you when it's three o'clock. That's when I want you to come home."

"Three o'clock?" Matt complained. "Why do I have to come home so early?"

"Three o'clock," Diana repeated.

"None of the other kids have to come in that early."

"You're pushing your luck, mister," Diana said.

"Okay, three o'clock. Can I go now?"

Diana gave him a kiss and ruffled his hair. "You can go."

She released the little boy and watched him dash off to his own bedroom. A great love welled up in her breast, and she had to swallow several times. In less than a minute Matt reappeared wearing his Incredible Hulk swim suit and clutching the Styrofoam bellyboard Kirby had given him.

"I'm going now," he announced.

"You won't forget?"

"Tell Guy I'm there, stay close to the tower," he repeated.

"And...?"

"And come home at three o'clock," Matt added reluctantly.

"You got it. Scoot along now."

Matthew dashed out of the house. Diana went into the living room and watched him through the window. He galloped to the corner, paused to pick a silvered dandelion, and blew the feathery seeds into the air. He rounded the corner heading toward the beach then, and was out of her sight.

Diana walked back into her studio and selected a brush. Before she could start again on the painting, the doorbell rang. She went out to answer it, and was surprised to find Kirby Franklin standing there.

"Hi," she said. "Playing hooky?"

Kirby did not respond to her smile. "I've been down at the chief of police's office. Some things have happened that you ought to know about."

A finger of fear touched her as she saw Kirby's grave expression. "What things?"

"Nancy Urich died last night."

"Oh, no! How did it happen?"

He passed over the question. "Philip Werhaus is dead too. His body was found last night."

Diana shivered. "Philip too? And there was Timmy and Edith, and now Nancy. Four people are dead all of a sudden. What's going on, Kirby? What's killing them?"

"I told you how Timmy died," he said. "As for the others, they just don't know. It's possible that it's some kind of rare disease."

Diana shook her head. "Oh, no. It isn't any disease, Kirby. It's the damned thing that's been following me.

It's after me, and because it hasn't been able to get me yet, it's killed those other people."

"Listen to what you're saying, Diana. That doesn't make any sense at all."

"I don't care if it makes sense or not," Her voice was rising, but she did not try to control it. "There's something evil here in Tranquilo Beach. Something that's not a part of this world at all. And whatever it is, it's after me!"

"Why don't you sit down?" Kirby said. "You're getting overexcited."

"Oh..." She looked around the room for something to shout at, then abruptly subsided. "Shit," she finished quietly. "I know I'm acting a little hysterical, but dammit, Kirby, this is a difficult time for me."

"I know it is," he said gently. "Let me get you a glass of wine."

"Why the hell not? Might as well be drunk as the way I am."

Kirby pointed down to her right hand. "Can I put that away for you?"

Diana was surprised to see she was still holding a Number 3 paintbrush. It was wet with a sick-looking yellow-gray acrylic.

"I have to rinse the paint off," she said.

"I'll do it," Kirby told her. "You sit down."

"Right, chief." She sank obediently into a chair and smiled up at him.

"That's better." Kirby carried the paintbrush up the short hall and disappeared into her studio. After a minute he was back, his face pale, the paintbrush still in his hand.

"What's the matter?" Diana asked, rising.

"That painting," he said, pointing back toward her studio. "What in the name of God is it?"

Diana stared at him wonderingly. "It's just an illustration for a children's book. See, there's this villain called Dr. Nose, and he builds a monster that is supposed to go around doing mischief to little children, but there's a mistake in the lab and the monster turns out to be a big, lovable, bumbling thing that can't do any harm to anybody. At least that's what I'm trying to come up with."

"Are you kidding me?"

"I am not kidding you." She took a step toward him. "Kirby, what's the matter?"

He searched her face for a moment, then said, "Come out here and take a look."

He walked back to her studio. Puzzled, Diana followed. At the door he stood aside and let her enter. Diana looked back at him questioningly, then turned and for the first time saw, really saw what she had painted.

"Oh, no!" she cried. "Oh, God, *no!*"

There on the posterboard that was mounted to her easel, painted in thick acrylic colors, was the scabrous creature that had haunted her dreams and her life since that terrible day in the fog. Every foul detail was there, exactly as she remembered.

Diana's stomach contracted without warning. She spun away and dashed across the hall to the bathroom. She reached the toilet just in time to vomit up the remains of her breakfast. After another minute of dry retching she rose shakily to her feet. Tactfully, Kirby had moved away from the doorway. When Diana came out into the hall he looked at her with an expression of deep worry.

"What is it, Diana?" he said.

"It's . . . the thing I told you about. My demon."

"But how could you paint it like that?"

"I didn't even know I was doing it, Kirby. It was a bigger shock to me than it was to you."

160

Kirby started to speak again, but Diana held up a hand. She cocked her head as though listening for something.

"I've got to go and get Matt," she said abruptly.

"Matt? What's the matter? Where is he?"

"He went down to the beach. And he's in danger."

Diana started past Kirby in the narrow hallway, but he put his hands on her shoulders to hold her.

"Let me go, dammit!"

"Settle down, Diana, you're talking crazy."

"Get out of my way, Kirby. My son is in danger and I have to go to him."

Surprised by her outburst, Kirby dropped his hands and stepped back. Diana ran past him and out the front door. After a moment he followed.

Diana ran all the way to the corner and turned, without pausing, for the beach. People strolling by stared at her—a wild-eyed woman in cut-off jeans and an outsized man's shirt, running crazily down the sidewalk.

She reached the low seawall and levered her legs across. For a moment she stood in the deep sand, shading her eyes from the sun, scanning the beach. There was a good-sized crowd in the surf and on the shore, but Diana did not see the little blond head she was looking for.

The chair in the lifeguard's tower was empty. Diana moved down closer to the water for another angle. Then, well up the beach, she caught the flash of red from the lifeguard's trunks. It was Guy Urich, and he was walking away from her. And beside him, holding tightly to Guy's hand, was Matthew.

21

"Matt!"

Diana's shout seemed to freeze all activity on the beach for an instant. Faces turned toward her, eyes wide with alarm. Even the seagulls stopped their incessant squawking for a moment and hovered in the air, watching.

Up the beach she saw Matthew stop and cock his head to listen. Guy leaned down to urge him on.

"Matt!" Diana called again. *"Wait!"*

She stumbled and fell forward in the deep sand. Cursing, she pulled off her sandals and threw them aside. She pushed herself erect and ran on barefoot.

Up ahead Matthew had not seen her yet. He had pulled his hand free of Guy's and was looking down the beach. Diana waved her arm in the air and he saw her. At the same moment Guy leaned down to say something to him.

Matt seemed to be torn between the two of them. Guy Urich, his friend and protector, was coaxing him on while his mother ran toward him, calling and waving.

The boy's moment of indecision passed. He shook his head no to Guy and ran back toward Diana.

She slowed down as the distance between them

closed. Her heart pounded with exertion and with relief. She looked up the beach once more to where Guy
Urich stood, long strong legs braced well apart. For a
subliminal moment she saw his face contorted into an
inhuman mask. Then, in less than the blink of an eye,
it was just the open, handsome face of the young lifeguard once more. He turned away from her and walked
off into the crowd of bathers.

When Matthew reached her, he had big tears in his
eyes. Diana bent down and swept the boy up in her
arms. She hugged him tightly to her.

"I didn't do anything," he said.

"I know, Matt. I know you didn't. I was frightened
and worried about you."

"You were worried about *me?*" he said.

She nodded wordlessly.

"I'm okay," he assured her. "Me and Guy were just
going to—"

"Matt, listen to me. I want you never, and I mean
never, to go anywhere with anybody without asking me
first if it's all right."

"Not even with Guy?"

"Especially not with Guy."

"But he's a lifeguard."

"I know, darling, and I just have to ask you to trust
me. It's something I can't talk about now. One of these
days you and I will sit down, and I'll explain the whole
thing to you. For now, just promise me you won't go
with anyone, no matter how well you know him, unless
you check with me. Okay?"

"Okay, I guess," Matt said.

"That's my big boy."

With Matt's little hand held tightly in her own,
Diana picked her way back across the beach to the
seawall. Kirby Franklin was there waiting for them.

"Is everything all right?" he asked.

"For now," she said.

"Is there anything I can do?"

"Thanks, Kirby, but I just have to be alone for a little while to sort all this out in my head."

"Fair enough," he said. "I'm going over to the Urichs'. I'll check back with you later."

She stood on tiptoe and kissed him lightly.

"Did you and Kirby have a fight?" Matt asked as the tall newspaperman walked away.

"No, dear. Let's go home."

When they were safely inside the cottage Diana locked the door. She opened a Pepsi for Matt, then sat down and lit a cigarette. She could not afford to stumble around blindly any longer. There had to be a plan of action.

The danger, she no longer had any doubt, was real and immediate. Something—some creature or being—was trying to get at her for reasons she did not know. To reach her it was invading the bodies of other people. There had been Edith Werhaus, Philip, and now very probably Guy Urich. And his sister too, if Diana had read her correctly the night before. Three of them were now dead. It appeared that once the thing had tried for her and missed, it moved on somehow to a new host body and abandoned the old one.

The thing that terrified her now was the new pattern whereby this thing, this devil, was trying to get at her through Matt. For herself Diana had the strength and the will to resist. Although she was pressed by both Edith and Philip she had not succumbed. And the fact that she recognized the change in Nancy early on may have saved her there. However, her little boy did not have her resources. If someone like Guy Urich, whom Matt liked and trusted, approached him, the boy

164

wouldn't suspect anything. Matthew was her Achilles' heel.

It was clear to Diana that she had to have help. She could not battle this thing alone, not with Matthew to worry about. Her impulse was to call on Kirby Franklin. Loyal, straight-ahead Kirby. Diana had no doubt that he would rally to her side. But Kirby was a practical man. He would offer natural explanations for happenings that could not be explained. This thing she was fighting did not operate in accordance with natural laws. She needed someone who could understand that.

Saul Julian.

The name jumped into her mind as though she had punched up the proper combination on a computer. The dark-eyed little mystic had seemed too far removed from reality when Diana had talked to him before. Or maybe it was simply that she did not want to believe what he had to tell her. Now she was out of options. She had no choice but to believe that the things that were happening around her had their origin in the occult. Saul Julian was the one man she knew who might be able to help.

She made immediate plans to drive into Santa Monica and talk to Julian. Then she remembered the encounter on the mountain road that had begun this nightmare, and she realized how vulnerable she was even locked inside a moving automobile. If she had to face the thing on the road again, she did not want Matthew with her. They had been lucky the last time to escape injury, or worse. She could not count on being that lucky again.

But where was she to leave Matt while she made the trip, ninety minutes up and ninety minutes back? Nancy Urich, the baby-sitter, was dead. If she asked Kirby, he would try to talk her out of going. Or he would insist on going with her. Either way, he would slow her down in doing what she had to do.

The only other possibility was Harriet Nagle. Things had been cool between Diana and Harriet since the fateful Saturday night at Edith's, but Diana still felt a strong bond of friendship for the woman. It had to be Harriet. There was no time to try to come up with somebody else.

"Matt," she called.

He came out of his bedroom carrying a *Mad* magazine.

"Wash your face, we're going over to Mrs. Nagle's."

"What for?"

"I have to go somewhere for a couple of hours, and I want you to stay with her."

"Can't I go along?"

"Not this time."

Matthew looked at her with sad eyes, and Diana realized she was asking him to do a lot without giving him any reasons.

"There's a fresh chocolate cake in the kitchen," she said. "We'll take it along to Mrs. Nagle's, and you can have all you want."

Matt brightened immediately. "Okay."

"Now make me happy and go wash your face."

While Matt splashed noisily in the bathroom, Diana sandwiched the hideous painting in an art folder and put it in the car. Then she went back inside and got Matt and the cake. She looked carefully up and down the street before driving off.

They found Harriet once again seated at the easel out in front of her art supply shop. She was working on the same off-kilter street scene. She looked up when Diana approached, surprised at first, then openly glad to see her.

166

The two women clasped hands. Their eyes said they had missed each other.

"It's good to see you," Harriet said.

"There are so many things I want to tell you," Diana said, "but right now I have to ask you for a favor."

"Ask away," Harriet said.

"Can you keep Matt with you for the rest of the afternoon?"

"I'll be glad to." Harriet looked at her friend more closely. "Are you in some kind of trouble?"

Diana looked nervously at the people strolling along the street. Normal, everyday people. She shivered. "Can we go inside?"

"Sure." Harriet opened the door, then gathered her easel, stool, and paints, and followed Diana and Matt into the cluttered little store.

Diana handed the cake to Matt. "Why don't you find a place to put this down?"

"Just a minute," Harriet said. She cleared a space on the counter for the cake, then found a sketchbook and a charcoal pencil among the jumbled merchandise. She turned them over to Matt, and soon he was happily smudging up the pages with charcoal renderings of stick men. Then the plump woman came back to join Diana.

"So what's happening?"

"Harriet, I'm going to have to ask you to take an awful lot on faith, but there just isn't time to explain now. I promise that when I get back I'll tell you the whole story."

"It better be good," Harriet said.

"You'll probably think I'm crazy."

"That's very possible. Meanwhile, what do you want me to do?"

"Keep Matt with you while I drive up to Santa Monica and back. I have to see someone there. It's very important. Keep Matt inside, and keep the door locked if you can."

"Keep the door locked?" Harriet repeated.

"Matt is in danger," Diana said. "Real physical danger. There are reasons why I don't want to take him with me now. When I get back I hope to have answers to some of the questions."

Harriet looked as though she were bursting with questions of her own, but she held them inside. "If you tell me he's in danger, that's good enough for me. There's a room in the rear of the shop where I sleep over sometimes. I'll lock up the shop and we'll wait back there for you. There are plenty of picture books around to keep Matt entertained."

"Harriet, you are a darling friend. There is no way I can tell you how much I appreciate this."

"Never mind that, but when you come back I expect a real juicy explanation of what the hell is going on around here."

"You got it," Diana promised. "I've got to run now. There isn't a lot of time."

The two women embraced for a moment, then Diana stepped back out the door onto the street. The green shade with CLOSED lettered across it rattled down on the inside of the glass door, and Diana heard the lock bolt shoot into place. She felt a rush of affection for her friend, and vowed to buy her a nice present when this was all over. Then she climbed into the Cutlass and headed out of town toward Interstate 5.

In the doorway of a sporting goods store across the street a tanned young man turned away from the window display of scuba gear and watched Diana drive off. Behind the dark glasses was the handsome young face of Guy Urich. But the mind and the body no longer belonged to the lifeguard.

In her little room at the rear of the shop Harriet cut a generous piece of cake for Matt and one for herself. She put a pan of water on the electric hot plate for instant coffee, and sat down to watch Matt cover the pages of the sketchbook.

Harriet was ready to burst with curiosity about what was going on with Diana. She could have pumped the little boy for information, but that was not her style. A friend had asked for help, and she had given it. Later, when Diana returned, she would tell Harriet the whole story. She had promised. The waiting would just make it all the more satisfying when she finally learned the facts.

She looked up as someone rattled the knob out at the front door.

Couldn't they see the CLOSED sign? Harriet wondered. The local people were accustomed to her irregular working hours, and accepted it as artistic eccentricity. It was probably some tourist, she thought, with an emergency need for a tube of chrome yellow.

Whoever it was stopped rattling the knob and banged on the door. A loud, insistent banging. There was a message of urgency in the knock. Nevertheless, Harriet remembered Diana's statement about the danger to Matt, and she resolved to let no one in.

The banging continued. Harriet decided it wouldn't hurt to at least go and take a peek at whoever it was. It was even possible that Diana had returned for something.

She stepped through the curtain that closed off the back room and walked toward the front of the shop. She kept close to one wall so whoever was outside would not see her through the show window. At the edge of the door there was a gap in the shade where she could look out.

Harriet put her eye to the gap and saw Guy Urich standing out in front. He looked worried.

Surely it wouldn't hurt to open the door to young Guy. There wasn't a more honest or better-liked boy in town than the blond young lifeguard. Still, she hesitated. Diana's fears had seemed very real.

"What is it?" she called through the door.

"Mrs. Nagle?"

"Yes. I'm closed for the day."

"It's Guy Urich, Mrs. Nagle. Can I come in for a minute?"

"I'm closed, Guy. What is it you wanted?"

"I just talked to Mrs. Cross. She gave me a message for you."

Well now, that was different, Harriet reasoned. If Diana sent him, then of course she should let him in. Maybe now she would get some hint of what this mystery was all about.

Harriet unlocked the door and Guy stepped into the shop. She pulled the door closed behind him.

"What's the message?" she asked.

Guy smiled at her. The smile was different from the All-American grin everyone knew. It was somehow insinuating. He said, "Is Matt here?"

"He's in the back room," Harriet said. "Is anything the matter, Guy?"

The young man reached out suddenly and took hold of her hands. It was something that Guy Urich would never have done. His hands, Harriet felt, were exceptionally warm, and very strong.

"You know, Mrs. Nagle," he said in a strange new voice, "I've always thought that you were a really nice-looking woman."

Harriet caught her breath. She could not believe that this was happening to her. And yet, here was the handsome young lifeguard standing very close to her, holding her hands tightly in his own, and saying these things to her.

"And for a long time," he continued, "I've had this really strong urge to kiss you."

Harriet found her voice at last. "Guy, what are you saying? I don't understand you."

"Yes, you do," he said. He wrapped his arms around her and pressed his firm young body against her yielding flesh. Harriet could feel the hardness of his sex. His hands massaged her back, sliding down over her full buttocks.

"Guy, don't," she said, but there was no conviction in her voice.

Then his mouth was on hers, his tongue forcing its way past her lips, caressing her own tongue. With a powerful effort of will she pulled her head away.

"Matt will see us," she whispered.

And then she didn't care any more. Guy's hands were inside her clothes, kneading the soft flesh of her most private places. Harriet relaxed and gave herself to him. The last thing she saw was the strange red glow of his eyes.

22

Diana accelerated down to the end of the main street of Tranquilo Beach without looking back. There she had to slow as two hundred Girl Scouts from the three Pacific states milled about the park, preparing for a campout. It was a reward for girls who had excelled in merit-badge competition. The eagerness and joy reflected in the girls' fresh young faces brought a lump to Diana's throat. Had there ever been a time when she was so happy? So innocent?

Once past the park, Diana speeded up again and dismissed the girls from her mind. She covered the five miles of blacktop to the interstate in as many minutes.

Once on the multilane highway she settled into a steady seventy-mile-an-hour pace. Well over the speed limit, but she would take her chances today with the Highway Patrol. She tuned the radio to an all-talk station in Los Angeles. The trivial opinions of strangers on trivial topics interested her not at all, but it served to keep her mind from dwelling on the horror that awaited her back in Tranquilo Beach. Or, God forbid, somewhere on the road up ahead.

In Orange County, Interstate 5 looped down around the southern section of Los Angeles before turning north again. When she came to Santa Monica Boulevard Diana pulled off the freeway and headed toward the ocean.

She pulled up in front of the little stucco bungalow where Saul Julian lived, and ran eagerly to the door. She knocked, then waited, chewing on a cuticle, for Julian to open the door. Nothing happened. She knocked again, more loudly. Nothing but silence from inside the house. In frustration Diana knocked again, and kept it up until she had to admit that Saul Julian simply was not at home.

How could he not be at home when she needed him so desperately? She raged inwardly at the little man, then caught herself and realized how irrational her anger was. With an effort she forced herself into a semblance of calm. She reviewed the situation.

All right, the man she had come to see was not available. There was nothing she could do about that. But as long as she had driven all the way up here, there were others she could call. When you needed help, you could not afford to be choosy.

She drove off and stopped at the first telephone booth she came to. It was an aluminum and glass box outside an Arco station. Diana parked the car and entered the booth. She dialed Jerry's office number. Odd, she thought, that she still knew it from memory when she could never recall the digits of her own license plate.

Jerry's secretary answered, crisp and professional. "Mr. Cross's office."

"I'd like to speak to him, please. This is Mrs. Cross."

There was a heartbeat's hesitation at the other end. "He's in a meeting right now, Mrs. Cross. May I have him call you when he's free?"

"No, you may not. This is extremely important. Please tell Mr. Cross that I have to talk to him right now."

"Hold on, please."

The tinkly music switched on as Diana was placed on hold. Waiting, she asked herself what the hell she was doing calling her ex-husband, anyway. She had not asked him for a thing since the divorce, and this would be a really rotten time to begin.

The music died abruptly and Jerry came on the line. "Yes, Diana, what is it?" Not very encouraging.

"There is, well, sort of a problem, Jerry."

"Oh, really? You can't mean that life in the artsy-craftsy beach town is not all beautiful."

"Could you skip the sarcasm? This is something serious, or I certainly wouldn't have called you."

"I'm sure it is," he said, "but try to understand that what I do here is serious too. Just now you had me pulled out of a meeting with the engineering manager and the vice president of sales."

"My God, the world will come to an end!"

"Now who's being sarcastic?"

"Are you trying to tell me that you don't have time for my problem?"

"I'm not saying that at all, Diana, but why can't I call you back when this is over? It shouldn't last more than another hour."

"You can't call me back, I'm in a telephone booth."

"Then you call me back. Listen, I've *got* to get back in there."

"Sure, Jerry, you go ahead." Diana replaced the receiver gently while Jerry's voice still chirped through the earpiece. She stood looking out through the glass at the cars driving in and out of the Arco station.

Her first impulse was to be angry at Jerry, but she knew that was not fair. Her problems were no longer his problems. She could have hooked him in by telling him Matthew was in danger, but that would be playing dirty. Besides, Jerry would seize the opportunity to remind her that he had opposed taking Matt to Tranquilo

Beach in the first place. Diana was not prepared to have to defend yet again her fitness to care for their son.

She considered trying Saul Julian again, but it had been just fifteen minutes since she'd left his empty house. Still, it would not hurt to give him a call. That's what she should have done in the first place. As she picked through her wallet for Julian's telephone number, Diana turned up the card of Dr. Alex Letterman. It made her focus on the irrational panic building up behind her forced calm. Since no one else was available, maybe the psychoanalyst could help. She dropped another coin into the telephone.

"Dr. Letterman?" she said, when they were connected. "This is Diana Cross."

"Ah, yes, Diana, how are you?" The doctor's deep, rich baritone was already comforting to her.

"As a matter of fact, I'm not so good," she said. "Is there any chance you could see me this afternoon?"

There was the slightest pause at the other end. "Is this an emergency, Diana?"

She started to deny it automatically, but instantly reminded herself that if this was not an emergency, she would never have one. She said, "Yes, doctor, this is an emergency."

"Then come right down to the office. I'll schedule you right in for a twenty-minute session."

"Thank you." Diana hung up the phone and was annoyed with herself for the excessive gratitude she felt to Dr. Letterman. He was, after all, her doctor, and it was not as though he were giving her something for nothing. Nevertheless, he had responded to her cry for help, and that was more than anyone else had done.

Diana drove to the new Century City complex and parked in the underground garage. She got out of the car, taking the art folder containing the painting with

175

her. The elevator carried her silently to the nineteenth floor, where Dr. Letterman's cool willowy receptionist was expecting her.

After ten minutes in the soothing surroundings of the doctor's waiting room, Diana was shown into the living-room-like office. Dr. Letterman greeted her warmly, and made no comment on the bulky art folder.

He listened impassively as she related the events of the past six weeks at Tranquilo Beach. She began with the dimly remembered Saturday night at Edith's house, and concluded with the inhuman flash of rage she had seen on the face of Guy Urich.

When she finished talking, Diana untied the ribbons that held the art folder closed and took out the painting that had turned into something quite different than she had intended.

Dr. Letterman's carefully controlled expression slipped into a grimace when he looked at the painting.

"God, it's ugly," he said. Then, remembering himself, he composed his features again.

"This is the thing that has been following me since that night on the mountain road," she said. "It has haunted my dreams, and I see sudden, unexplainable flashes of it in people I know."

"Did you paint the picture?" Letterman asked.

"I'd have to say my subconscious painted it. I thought I was doing an illustration for a children's book."

He stared at the picture for a moment longer. "Would you mind putting it away?"

Diana slipped the painting back into the folder and knotted the tie ribbons.

The doctor settled himself into the soft leather chair and gazed benignly across the coffee table at Diana. "Tell me, does that painting remind you of anyone?"

"Do you mean of a human being?"

"Yes, of course."

"Hardly. And yet, in an odd, frightening way, there is something familiar about it. I felt it that night in the fog, and again at the séance. I feel it now when I look at the picture. It's like something way, way back in a dusty corner of my memory."

Letterman tapped his fingers together. "Mm-hmm. And how does it make you feel, Diana, when you get this sense of familiarity?"

"It makes me feel scared shitless, if you want to know the truth."

"I see." Dr. Letterman got up and strolled across the room to a wall bookcase. He pressed a concealed release and a section of book backs swung away to reveal a well-stocked medicine cabinet. He selected a bottle of flat blue tablets and shook several of them into a small envelope. He sealed the envelope and carried it back to Diana.

"Take one of these after meals and before you go to bed," he said.

Diana took the envelope from him and shook it lightly. "What is it?"

"Valium, ten milligrams."

"A tranquilizer? I come to you with the biggest trouble I have ever had in my life, and all you have to offer me is a tranquilizer?"

"It's a stopgap measure only," said Letterman. "I advise against any long-term use of tranquilizers."

"The hell with stopgap," Diana said. "I need something that will put an end to this nightmare I'm living."

"Do you want my honest opinion?" the doctor asked.

"Of course I do."

"If we had a situation of ongoing treatment here, I would not be as blunt as I am about to be. But you are here only because of an emergency, so I must assume I will not see you soon again. Therefore, I will condense the message. Diana, I feel you are a seriously disturbed

177

woman. My advice to you, based on your condition as I perceive it, is to seek inpatient psychotherapy."

Diana stared at him "Inpatient psychotherapy? Does that mean you think I should commit myself to a mental institution?"

"Again, bluntly stated, I think that would be the best step you could take at this time."

Diana stood up. She clutched the art folder to her, leaving the package of pills lying on the table.

"Thank you, Dr. Letterman. Or I suppose I should make that Alex. You were always very big with first names. It's been very enlightening to chat with you here in your make-believe living room. Naturally, I expect you to bill me for a full hour. But, Alex, if you think I am going to sign myself into the booby hatch because you can't do anything to help me, forget it."

"Diana...Mrs. Cross, I—"

"Never mind, doctor, my twenty minutes is up. I'm sure you have another sick mind waiting."

Diana turned away from him. With as much dignity as she could manage, she marched out of his office, past the willowy receptionist, and down the deep-carpeted hall to the elevator. She rode down to the parking level, retrieved her car, and drove out onto Pico Boulevard before the tears came.

She had to pull over to the curb for a minute and use a Kleenex to dab at her eyes and blow her nose. Bitter frustration rose in her throat like bile.

"Goddam sonofabitch!" she said through clenched teeth. "Whatever you are, you ugly, stinking piece of garbage, hear this...I will not give up." Somehow, having said that, she felt better.

Out on the sidewalk several pedestrians had stopped and were looking at her curiously. She gave them a smile and a merry wave, then put the car in gear. She headed back toward Santa Monica to try one more time to reach Saul Julian.

This time when she pulled up at the bungalow there was a white MGB with the top down parked in the driveway.

Let it be his car, Diana said silently. *Please let him be home.*

Carrying the art folder under her arm, Diana hurried from her car to the front door of the bungalow. She knocked loudly, and as the seconds ticked by, she felt the creeping return of despair. Then abruptly the door swung open and Saul Julian stood there looking out at her.

"Diana, how good to see you again. Come on inside."

"Saul, I'm so glad you're here."

"How can I help you?"

"First, you might assure me that I'm not crazy, because that's what I've just been told by a man with the credentials that allow him to say that."

"You're not crazy," said Julian. "Have a chair."

When they were seated in the comfortable, cluttered living room, Diana went over the same ground she had covered with Dr. Letterman. Julian listened intently, his bright little eyes never leaving her face. He brushed one hand repeatedly through his bristle of black hair. When she had finished the story, Diana sat back and waited for his reaction.

Julian nodded at the folder. "Are you going to show me the picture?"

Diana untied the ribbons and pulled out the acrylic painting. She held it up for Julian to see.

"Jesus." He released a long exhalation. "It's hideous."

"That's approximately what Dr. Letterman said," Diana told him.

"He has a good eye."

Julian took the posterboard from Diana and propped it up in a chair. He backed off several steps and stood looking at it. He cocked his head to one side, then to the other.

"I've seen this sucker before," he said.

"Have you?" Diana leaned forward anxiously.

"Somewhere...somewhere." Julian scrubbed at his skullcap of hair. "I just can't remember where."

"Then it isn't something out of my mind?"

"No, of course it isn't," he said with a touch of impatience. "I told you that when you were here before. I wanted to work with you then, if you remember."

"I remember," she said quietly. "I should have listened to you."

He waved it aside. "That's not important now. What you have here in this picture is bad business, Diana. Very bad. It doesn't take a psychic to look at the thing and tell that. The important thing I can tell you now is that this is real. The danger to you and those close to you is very real."

"I was sure of it," Diana said, "but it's reassuring to have someone else say so too."

"What you have to do now," Julian said emphatically, "is fight."

Diana gestured toward the painting that occupied its chair like an unwelcome guest. "Fight *that*? Are you serious?"

"I am deadly serious. It's your only chance. You have the power, Diana, I told you that before. I've never met anyone who carries a stronger psychic aura than you do."

"I'm afraid, Saul."

"You'd be a fool if you weren't afraid. But you don't have to fight alone. I can help you because I have the knowledge and the experience. But the power to defeat this thing has to come from you."

"I don't feel very powerful."

"Take my word for it, you are. But the power won't do you a damn bit of good if you won't use it."

Diana looked at the loathsome beast she had painted. She felt cold. "All I want is to get away from *that*."

"You can't run away from it," Julian said.

"Now you sound like Dr. Letterman."

"In a way we're in the same line of work. He deals with the devils of the mind, I deal with the devils that exist in the dark corners of the real world. I know what I'm talking about, Diana. Running will not help."

She sagged against the upholstered back of the love seat. "It seems like such an unequal battle."

"Do you trust me?" Julian asked.

Diana looked into the small man's bright, eager eyes. "I trust you, Saul."

"I want you to stay here and wait for me while I go to see someone."

"I don't understand."

"This person has the finest collection of authentic books on the occult I have ever seen. It may take me a while, but using those books I'm sure I can identify that thing in your painting."

"How will that help?" Diana asked.

"Once we know exactly what we're up against, we'll know the best way to fight it."

Diana started to respond, then stood up suddenly and walked to the window. She peered out into the dusk as though she had heard something out there.

"I can't stay, Saul. I left my little boy with a friend in Tranquilo Beach. I have a strong feeling that he needs me. I must go to him."

Julian stood up and studied her. "If you have that feeling, Diana, then by all means go. Be very careful."

"I will," she said absently.

"Leave me a phone number where I can get in touch with you."

Diana wrote down the number of the telephone she'd had put in at the cottage. "This is where I'm living, but I'm not sure I'll be there."

"Is there another place? It may be very important that I get to you."

"Harriet's Art Supplies. It's a little store in the middle of the main street. Harriet Nagle is the friend I left Matt with."

Julian wrote down the name. "Do you mind if I keep the painting here?"

"Lord no. Keep the damned thing as long as you want." Diana edged toward the door. "Saul, I'm sorry, but I have to get back there."

"I understand," he said.

They walked together out to Diana's car. Saul Julian stood alone and watched her drive away until she was out of sight.

23

Julian walked slowly in from the street when Diana had gone and sat in a chair facing the one with the painting. For many minutes he stared at the creature depicted there. The vivid acrylic colors shifted and swam before his eyes as the thing seemed to shift like a fetus impatient for birth.

With sudden resolve Julian pushed himself out of the chair and went into the second bedroom of the bungalow, the room he used as a study. From a bookcase there he drew a volume on the origins of witchcraft and demonology. He leafed quickly through the pages, then slammed the book shut and took out another. He gave this one only a cursory look before returning it to the shelf.

He was wasting his time in here, Julian realized. He had read all these books many times. If the creature in Diana's painting were in any of his own books, he would have recognized it immediately. He would have to go to the Duchess.

He had planned to wait until morning to visit the Duchess. It was not a pleasant prospect after dark. However, being left alone with the grisly painting had given him a strong sense of urgency.

He carried the posterboard out and slid it carefully

183

into the cramped space behind the seats of the MG. Then he got in, keyed the little engine to life, and drove the few miles south along the Pacific to Venice.

Venice, California, was conceived as a kind of movie-set version of Venice, Italy. There were canals with real gondolas, humpbacked footbridges, buildings with Byzantine-style fronts of plaster and chicken wire. Then the stock market plummeted and the money drained out of Venice faster than the water from the Grand Canal. The town was annexed by Los Angeles and rapidly deteriorated into a seaside slum. In the 1950s the beatnik movement found a home in the seedy coffee houses, and artists could rent storefront studios cheaply. A decade later the hippies and their drugs squeezed the artists out. In the 1970s Venice was rediscovered by real estate developers, and high-rise condominiums with prices to match went up along the choice beachfront. However, not far inland there remained narrow streets that the wary pedestrian avoided after dark.

One such street was Medici Place. There, between a burned-out movie theater and a used-clothing shop, was the unpainted, unnamed store operated by the Duchess.

Saul Julian pulled up and parked in front of the store. He took the painting from behind the seat and carried it across the littered sidewalk to the windowless door. He twisted the old-fashioned bell key set into the center of the panel and waited. After ninety seconds he heard shuffling footsteps and the tap of a cane inside. It was another minute before the locks rattled free and the door opened to the six inches allowed by the chain.

The face of an ancient black woman, wrinkled like a walnut, peered out at him.

"What you want?"

"It's Saul Julian, Duchess. I want to take a look at your books."

"Just lookin', not buyin'?"

"If you have what I want, I'll buy it," he said. "This is important, Duchess."

"Hmmph! It's always important."

The door closed in his face, and for a moment Julian thought the old woman had gone away. Then the chain slid out and the door opened again, just enough to allow Julian inside.

The floor of the narrow store was littered with papers, cans, bits of string and wire, and little gray things that Julian carefully stepped across. Shelves along one wall and a counter at the rear held bottles of all sizes containing liquids in various colors and densities. There were polished bones, packets of powders, chicken feet, boars' ears, medals, charms, amulets, and many other unidentifiable but vaguely disturbing items. One entire wall was books. Old books, soiled books, torn books, forbidden books. Books that could be found nowhere else. Presiding over the confusion, on a perch above the door, was a mummified monkey. And looking very much like a mummy herself was the Duchess.

If she had a name, it was long ago forgotten. No one called her anything but the Duchess. She was, by various estimates, somewhere between 80 and 110 years old. Her mouth was toothless, her back bent into a question mark. The bones of her hands and arms were clearly defined under the withered black skin. She moved in painful little steps with the aid of a blackthorn cane. But it was her eyes that people remembered. They were black and shiny as polished grapes. The whites were clear and unveined. The eyes missed nothing.

"What you want from my books, ghost chaser?" the

old woman said. Her voice was like a hot wind through dried palms.

Julian held up Diana's painting for the old woman to see. "I want to learn about this."

The Duchess looked at the picture with no change of her expression.

"Astragoth," she said.

Julian smacked his forehead. "Yes, that's the name. Do you have a book that will tell me about him?"

The remarkable eyes regarded him brightly. "You don't want to mess with Astragoth."

"I'm not messing with anything, Duchess, I just want to learn. Do you have the book?"

"I got it."

Julian waited for the old woman to continue, but she merely leaned on her cane and watched him with her shiny black eyes.

"Can I see it?" he asked finally.

"Won't do you no good."

"Please, Duchess, the book." Julian wanted to grab the old woman by the frail shoulders and shake her, but he knew better. If the Duchess wanted you to have something, she would give it to you or sell it to you. If not, no amount of money could buy it.

At last she shook her old head and turned away from him. Tap-tapping with the cane, she shuffled across the room to the wall of books. She raised the stick and pointed to a rat-bitten leather volume on a high shelf.

Julian walked over to her side, reached up and took down the old book. The title, stamped into the cover long ago, was barely legible now.

Daemons of the Olde Worlde.

Julian leafed carefully through the ragged pages. He stopped suddenly as one of the illustrations seemed to jump out at him.

It was a woodcut showing a loathsome beast that

was unquestionably the same one Diana had painted from her subconscious memory. The creature held in its talons the limp figure of a pale-haired woman while it engaged in a foul act of sex. Julian was stunned by the resemblance of the woman in the old illustration to Diana Cross. The caption under the picture read: *Astragoth Claims His Bride.*

"You want the book?" the old woman asked.

"Yes, I'll take it. How much?"

"Hundred dollars."

"For this old piece of trash? Look at it, the spine's cracked, the pages are falling out."

"You don't want the book, put it back."

"No, I'll take it," Julian said. He took out his checkbook and made room on the splintery counter to write. "But you're holding me up."

"Hundred dollars won't make no difference to you," said the Duchess.

Julian stopped writing and looked up at her. "Why do you say that?"

"Hundred dollars, thousand dollars, it don't make no difference to you now."

Looking into the old woman's eyes, he felt a momentary chill. Quickly he signed his name to the check, tore it out and gave it to her. He had gone too far to let himself be spooked by an ancient black woman in a shabby occult store.

He took the book back to the bungalow in Santa Monica. There he read carefully the section on the demon Astragoth. It was difficult reading with the archaic language and the obscure typeface, but in less than an hour he knew all he had to know. With a red pen he underlined the important passages, then carried the book out to his little MG. He sped south after Diana Cross, hoping he was not too late.

With every mile she cut from the distance between her and Tranquilo Beach Diana grew more anxious. Something down there was dreadfully wrong. Matthew was in danger. These messages came through as clearly as though they had been broadcast over the car radio. To keep from crying aloud she forced all of her attention on the unreeling pavement as she drove through the gathering dusk.

The last glimmer of daylight drained away as she turned off the freeway onto the road to Tranquilo Beach. By the time she pulled into the town it was night. The streets were already damp with a mist from the sea.

Driving past the park, Diana could see the orange flicker of campfires through the trees. The treble laughter of the Girl Scouts floated to her through the night. In a small part of her mind Diana envied the girls their untroubled young lives. Then she pushed the thought away and drove on down the street to Harriet Nagle's art shop.

The front of the store was dark, and Diana felt a prickling at the back of her neck. She parked the car and got out. The street was deserted on both sides, except for half a dozen isolated strollers. Diana's heels rang on the wet pavement as she crossed the sidewalk to the door of the shop. The green shade with CLOSED printed across it was still pulled down inside the glass.

Why was there no light showing from inside? she wondered. Why was there no sound? A radio or television set should have been playing. Something.

Diana rapped her knuckles against the cold glass of the door. She slapped the wood frame with the flat of her hand. Nothing stirred inside.

Without waiting any longer, Diana grasped the brass handle and depressed the thumb latch. The door swung open to her touch. In the shadows beyond the door lay something evil. The fine hairs on her forearms bristled. Every instinct told her to go away from there. But there was no turning back. Her little boy was in danger. She stepped through the door into the shop.

Carefully Diana felt her way through the stacked cartons and piles of artists' supplies to the curtain that closed off the room in the rear. As she moved back the familiar hateful stench assaulted her.

When she found the curtain Diana pushed it cautiously aside and stepped into the room. No light from the street lamps outside penetrated here. She closed her eyes and tried to visualize the layout as she remembered it. There should have been a wall fixture with a chain just to the right of the entrance. Diana fought down the impulse to gag at the stink of putrefaction. She reached out and felt along the wall until she found the chain. She pulled it and the orange-shaded light clicked on.

Once this had been a pleasant enough little room. It had a comfortable chair, a small television set, a sink, a hot plate, a few dishes neatly stacked on a shelf, and a narrow studio bed. There was nothing pleasant about the room now. It was filled with death.

Lying naked on the bed, face up, one hand trailing

on the floor, was Guy Urich. His muscular lifeguard's body looked shriveled and collapsed, his rich tan gone yellow. The staring eyes were sunk deep into their sockets. The mouth gaped.

Diana groaned and pulled her eyes away from the young man's body. She looked quickly around the room for any sign of Matthew or Harriet, but found none. The panic started to rise in her throat. She clenched her fists and breathed slowly, deeply, until she was in control of herself again.

She walked back and pulled the light chain, returning the room to darkness. She eased past the curtain and picked her way back through the shop guided by the light that filtered through the front window. She opened the door and stepped out onto the street. A couple in their late fifties, looking comfortably married, strolled past. They smiled at her. Diana's face twisted reflexively into an unconvincing answering smile. The couple were too wrapped up in themselves to notice anything strange in her behavior.

Diana leaned for a moment against the wall of the building, letting her hands press against the grainy surface of the stone. When she regained some of her composure she walked on to the end of the block. There, outside the Thrifty Drug Store, were a pair of pay telephones in their plastic acoustic shells. Diana picked up the receiver of the nearest phone, dropped a coin into the slot, and punched out the number of the *Tide* office.

Olive Quinlan, a pleasant middle-aged woman, who was the only full-time employee besides Kirby Franklin, answered.

"Hello, Olive," Diana said, striving to keep her voice level. "Is Kirby there?"

"Oh, hi, Diana. No, he isn't. He and Chief Ratcher went down to Oceanside with that Dr. Sussman. It has something to do with the mysterious deaths we've been

190

having. Isn't it exciting? I mean, it's awful and scary and all that, but it *is* exciting."

"Do you have an idea when Kirby will be back?" Diana asked when Olive paused for breath.

"Not really, but he'll probably stop back here at the office before he goes home. We had another one, did you hear?"

"What?" Diana said distractedly.

"Another of those weird deaths. Nancy Urich, you know her. They found her dead in her bed. Nobody has any idea what's causing it."

"Yes, it's a terrible thing. Look, Olive, I have to go now, but I'd like you to ask Kirby to get in touch with me as soon as he comes back. It's very important."

"Sure, be glad to. Is there anything you want me to tell him?"

"No, nothing else. Thanks, Olive." Diana hung up the phone before the other woman could resume the conversation. The last thing she wanted to do right now was chat about the mysterious epidemic that was attacking Tranquilo Beach people.

She walked back down the street and got into her car in front of Harriet's shop. The damp chill of the air made her shiver. The word CLOSED in block letters on the green window shade in the shop's front door had an air of deadly finality. Diana looked away. The proper, normal thing to do now would be to call the police and report her discovery of Guy Urich's body. But this was hardly a normal situation. If she called the police they would ask her a lot of questions for which she had no answers. Her main concern now— her *only* concern—was to find little Matthew before it was too late.

Diana started the car and reached for the shift lever, then realized she had no idea where she should go next. She closed her eyes and concentrated. Somewhere out there in the darkness were her little boy and her friend Harriet. The possibilities were limitless, making it foolish to rush off without a destination. The only place to go now that made any sense was her cottage. There she would be among familiar things, and perhaps better able to come up with a plan. She put the car in gear and drove off; trying to keep the dark out of her mind.

When she pulled up to park on the street out in front of her cottage she could see a pale rectangle that did not belong there at eye level on the dark wood of the door. She left the car with the motor idling and ran across the lawn. The pale rectangle proved to be a folded sheet of white notepaper thumbtacked to the door. She yanked the paper free and opened it out. In the glow from the car's headlights she recognized Harriet's softly rounded script. She flattened the note against the door panel and read it.

Diana—
 We've got bad trouble. I'm taking Matt up to Edith's house. We need you. For Matt's sake come alone. Explanations later.

Harriet

Bad trouble: Edith's house? Why was there no mention of Guy Urich? The questions tumbled through Diana's mind, but she could not wait for the answers. She ran back to the car, jerked into a U-turn, and drove off.

When she reached the old house where Edith Werhaus had lived Diana saw Harriet Nagle's battered station wagon parked at the foot of the steps that led to the door. She left her own car behind the station wagon and went quickly up the steps. When she reached the top she saw that the front door was slightly ajar. Somewhere inside the house a dim light glimmered. Without

192

hesitation Diana pushed the door open and stepped in.

"There you are!"

Diana's knees jellied at the sudden sound of a voice. She spun around, then almost cried with relief when she saw Harriet coming toward her.

"My God, you scared me."

"Diana, I'm so glad you're here."

The plump woman embraced her. Diana returned the hug for a moment, then pulled back. "What's going on, Harriet? Where's Matt?"

"Come on downstairs," Harriet said. "We've got to hurry." She began to pull Diana toward the kitchen, from where the stairway led down to the basement.

Diana held back. "Is Matt downstairs? What's he doing down there?"

"There isn't time to explain now," Harriet said, tugging at her arm.

Diana allowed herself to be led through the house until they stood at the top of the narrow stairway to the basement. The mustiness of the old house oppressed her. It seemed to have been closed up for years. The whole thing seemed wrong to her, but if Matthew needed her, she could not stop to worry about it. Harriet started down the steps. Diana followed.

"This way," Harriet called, urging her on. "There isn't much time."

It was cold in the basement. Cold as the grave. Harriet led her past the old furnace and into the recreation room. Right here the horror had begun. It seemed to Diana very long ago, but was not yet two weeks.

"Where are we going, Harriet? Where is my boy?"

The stocky woman hurried on without answering. Diana followed more slowly now, and came to a stop when she saw where Harriet had chosen to stand. It was in the center of the pentagram painted on the floor of the recreation room. With a shock Diana saw that five black candles burned again at the points of the star. Then Harriet turned to face her.

The features all belonged to the Harriet Nagle Diana knew, but the expression was something else. It was a look of wild, inhuman triumph that could never have fit on the soft, friendly face. Harriet began to laugh.

"Who are you?" Diana demanded. "What are you? What have you done with my little boy?"

In short, subliminal flashes Diana now saw the thing that lived in the body of Harriet Nagle. It was the monstrous creature from the fog, the one that had appeared in her painting, the thing that had made Diana's life a hell. Then it was Harriet again. Or at least the semblance of Harriet.

The mouth opened, but the voice that came out belonged to nothing that lived on earth. It was a rough, deep growl without human quality.

"I...am...Astragoth."

Diana shook her head. "That has no meaning for me." She blinked, trying to keep the Harriet face in focus. "Why are you doing this to me?"

"You are my bride," the voice rumbled. "Now I claim my rights."

"I am no one's bride," Diana said. "You have no rights over me."

Harriet thrust out an arm, pointing at her. Before Diana's eyes the forefinger lengthened into a scaly talon.

"You cannot refuse. You are lawfully given to me. Through the ages I have waited to be called back to earth. Now I am here. Now I claim my bride."

The scene wavered before Diana's eyes. She fought down a surge of nausea and braced herself to face the thing that wore the body of her friend.

"Where is my son?"

"I have him, but I have spared him until now. Once

you are my bride in fact and in flesh, I will release him."

"What have you done to him?"

The Harriet lips stretched into an ugly smile. "I have done him no harm...yet."

Diana pinched her eyes closed. All through her life, with the recurring experiences of ESP, she had never consciously tried to make contact with another mind. She tried now. She put every ounce of her will into the effort. *Matthew!* her mind cried out. *Matthew! Matthew!*

At first there was only silence and darkness. Then, faintly, the sound of a child crying. Her child. Matthew was somewhere unable to move. There was water all around him. This much Diana could sense.

"You can do nothing to help him," said the terrible voice.

Diana opened her eyes to see Harriet reaching out to her. In strobelike flashes she saw the fingers as claws encrusted with filth.

"Come to me," the demon voice urged. "Give yourself to me and the boy will be spared."

Diana felt the will to resist being sucked out of her. She took a faltering step toward the center of the pentagram where Harriet waited. Then, in sudden clarity of memory, she saw the vile performance that had been played out in this room the last time she was here. Edith Werhaus bent over, legs spread apart, clutching the lectern with both hands while the beast ravaged her.

"No," she said in a clear, firm voice. "You lie. I will make no bargain until I see my son."

The Harriet face distorted into a furious mask. "Bargain? Astragoth makes no bargains with mortals. You belong to me. Come willingly to me now, or I will take you by force."

Diana stood frozen as the Harriet thing started toward her. She was torn by conflicting emotions. First there was the powerful impulse to run. Flee up the stairs and out of this accursed house. Somehow get away in the night from this creature that had taken her friend's body. But deeper than the fear was the knowledge that she must stand and fight. Fight for herself and for her son. Diana tried to will strength into her unwilling body as the thing with Harriet's face came closer.

25

Saul Julian kept his foot heavy on the accelerator and pushed the little MG south on Interstate 5. The snarl of the four-cylinder engine and the rush of wind filled his ears. The night all around him seemed full of demons. Beside him on the passenger seat lay the book he had bought from the Duchess. Tucked behind the seats was Diana's terrible painting.

He came at last to the green-and-white freeway sign for the Tranquilo Beach off-ramp. He peeled off and sped the last five miles on the two-lane road as his stomach cramped with anxiety.

Julian drove past the park where the coals of a few campfires still glowed outside the tents of the sleeping Girl Scouts. There seemed to be no sound in the entire town. He drove on to the first of the town's two traffic lights and stopped while he dug into his pocket for a scrap of paper with Diana's telephone number written on it. Before he found it, his attention was taken by the flashing red light of a police car in the next block.

He let the car roll forward and eased over to the curb. The sign over the shop where all the activity was read: *Harriet's Art Supplies*. A thickset man in a blue police uniform seemed to be in charge. He looked over suspiciously at Saul and walked slowly toward the car, mopping his face with a handkerchief.

"You have business here, mister?"

"I'm looking for a woman named Diana Cross," Julian said.

At the mention of Diana's name a tall young man in a tweed jacket turned away from his conversation with the ambulance driver and came over.

"I'm Kirby Franklin," he said. "Are you a friend of Diana's?"

"Yes. My name is Saul Julian. I'm from Los Angeles."

"Oh yes, the mystic."

"Psychic," Julian corrected.

"Right. Did you have something important to talk to Diana about?"

"Very important. Diana is in deep trouble. I don't think she knows how deep. Can you tell me how to find her?"

"I can ride out to her place with you if you'll wait a minute while I call my office."

"Sure," Julian said. "I'd appreciate the company."

Kirby made his phone call and came back to the car wearing a puzzled frown. "Diana left word for me to call her. She didn't say why, but I don't like the sound of it."

"Let's go."

Saul pushed open the door of the little car and Kirby jackknifed himself into the passenger seat, picking up the book as he got in. He tilted the ragged volume so he could read the title in the glow of a street lamp.

"*Daemons of the Olde Worlde*. Does this book have anything to do with Diana?"

"I'm afraid it does," Julian said. "Can I explain on the way to her place?"

"Head on down the street in the direction you were

oing, and I'll tell you when to turn left." Kirby looked
up at the uniformed man who was standing by uncertainly. "I'll check with you later, Bo."

Julian drove the MG down the deserted main street
of Tranquilo Beach. The neat little commercial district
was quickly behind them, and they entered a stretch
of well-kept, comfortable-looking houses.

"What was going on back there?" Julian asked.

"A boy from the town here died in a very strange
way. Has Diana told you anything about what's happening here?"

"A little. She showed me the painting."

"God, that awful thing. Did it mean anything to
you?"

Julian reached over and tapped the book that Kirby
still held in his lap. "Open it to the page I have marked.
Take a look at the picture there."

Kirby cracked open the old book and peered down
at the woodcut, *Astragoth Claims His Bride.* He looked
over at Julian, his face pale under the newly risen
moon. "That . . . creature . . . it's the same as in Diana's
painting."

Julian nodded. "Did she ever talk to you about her
demon?"

"Well, yes, but I didn't pay much attention at the
time."

"You'd better pay attention now," Julian said, "because the thing she painted, the thing you see there in
that old illustration, is Diana's demon. Somehow it has
returned to earth, and it's come for her. And it is going
to take her unless we can do something damned fast."

Kirby looked again at the ugly woodcut and shuddered. "This is an awful lot for a rational man to accept
all at once." He looked out to see where they were.
"Turn left at the next street."

Julian spun the MG into the corner. "I know this is

hard as hell to believe coming on cold, but if we're going to help Diana, you've got to take my word for it. Later on we can go into the whole story in depth."

"Left again here," Kirby directed. "It's the cottage set back from the street."

Saul slid to a stop on the street in front of the little house. No lights showed through the windows. Kirby jumped out of the car and ran up the short path to the front door. Julian followed. Kirby was pounding on the door by the time he got there.

"Diana! Diana, are you in there? It's Kirby."

There was no answer from inside. Kirby tried the door and found it locked. While Kirby rattled the knob, Julian stooped to pick up something white from the ground near the door. It was a crumpled ball of note paper. He smoothed it out and showed it to Kirby.

"What do you make of this?"

Kirby scanned the handwritten message. "It's a note to Diana from Harriet Nagle. There's some kind of trouble, and she's taken Diana's little boy to a house out on the cliff highway."

"Would Diana have gone there?"

"Definitely, if she read this note."

"Then we'd better get there as fast as possible."

The two men sprinted back to the MG and Julian peeled away from the curb. He kept the accelerator floorboarded as he followed Kirby's directions, skidding the little car out of the town and north along the narrow cliff road. They pulled up in front of the steps leading up to the dark old structure where the Werhaus family had lived.

"It looks empty," Julian said.

"Diana's car is here. Harriet's too. And there at the basement window you can see a flicker of light."

The two men trotted up the steps to the front door

chilled through their clothing by the light wind off the sea. The door stood ajar when they reached it. For a moment they paused as the fetid odor hit them. Then they plunged into the house.

26

The thing that lived in Harriet Nagle's body came closer to Diana. The plump flesh twisted and squirmed on its face, as though trying to tear loose from the skull. The teeth and the bright-pink gums were bared in a wide grimace.

Diana stood her ground. She choked down the impulse to flee and recalled the words of Saul Julian: *You can't run away from it. . . . You must fight. . . . You have the power!*

The power. Diana tried to feel it within herself. All her life she had struggled against the strange force that set her apart from other people. She had denied its very existence. Now she called upon that force to make her strong. She needed the power now in a battle for her life.

The thing called Astragoth came toward her.

I must fight! Diana told herself. She stood braced, legs apart, and faced the oncoming creature. She stabbed a forefinger at the beast's face.

"No!" she cried. "You will not have me!"

The Harriet thing faltered and came to a stop. The eyes glowed hot and red. "You cannot defy Astragoth!"

"I do defy you!" Diana said, fighting for control of her voice.

The creature spread its arms wide and roared through the gaping Harriet mouth. Its rumbling bellow filled the wood-paneled basement room like an explosion.

Shock waves hammered at Diana, each more powerful than the last. Tears dimmed her vision, her head ached, she wanted to vomit. But she stood her ground.

You have the power, Julian's voice echoed in her mind. *Only you.*

"Foolish mortal woman," thundered the demon voice. "You cannot oppose Astragoth!"

A blast of superheated wind struck Diana as though she stood before an open-hearth furnace. Light more brilliant than a laser pierced her eyes, and for a moment she was blinded.

Summoning all of her strength, calling on the psychic force she had so long denied, Diana raised her arms in a gesture of command. She tore the words from her throat in a defiant shout:

"I have the power!"

Incredibly, the creature flinched. The face twisted into a hideous mask of rage.

Still half-blinded and with the hot wind searing her face, Diana took a step forward.

"I have the power," she said again. Her voice was firm now, and it crackled with newfound energy.

The scorching wind stopped suddenly. The pain in Diana's head drained away. The demon shuddered and took a step backward. Diana advanced another step.

She felt herself growing stronger with every heartbeat. She could sense victory. Then a sudden noise somewhere behind her, voices shouting, and the powerful concentration of energy Diana had built up was dissipated. She turned and looked as Kirby and Saul Julian pounded into the room. An unholy flash of triumph crossed the face of the demon.

Diana fought to regain her lost momentum, but the battle had sapped her strength, and the sudden distraction had taken away her advantage. The outlines of the room faded and wobbled. The figures of the demon and the two onrushing men blurred. A curtain of black came down and Diana fell.

27

Cold.

The first sensation to come to Diana as consciousness returned was that she was cold. Her hand reached down automatically for the blanket she kept folded across the foot of the bed. Instead of the soft cloth, her fingers scraped against a hard foreign surface. Diana opened her eyes and blinked several times before full awareness returned. She was lying on the cold, unyielding floor of Edith Werhaus's basement recreation room. And she was not alone.

She rose shakily to her feet. Two of the black candles that had burned in the points of the pentagram had guttered out. In the flickering light of the three that still burned Diana saw two bodies lying crumpled on the floor.

Cautiously Diana approached the still form that lay nearest to her. The drawn, empty-eyed face of Harriet Nagle looked up at her. The spirit of the demon was gone. Harriet had found peace at last.

Diana left her and walked over to the other body. Saul Julian looked very small and still lying there on the cold floor of the basement room. Diana felt a sharp pang of sorrow for the little man.

Saul groaned.

Diana jumped back, then knelt quickly by his side and took his hand. She chafed the thin wrist, trying to will the blood to circulate.

Julian opened his eyes and blinked. He struggled to sit up.

"Diana, are you all right?"

"Yes. What are you doing here?"

"I found a book with your demon in it. Astragoth. I came to warn you. Kirby Franklin and I—"

He broke off, swiveling his head to look around the room. His eyes fell on the sucked-out body of Harriet Nagle.

"Where's Kirby?" he said.

"I don't know. I saw him come in with you, then I guess I passed out."

"We came into the room together," Julian said. "I was right behind him. We saw you and that...that creature, and both of us yelled. We ran at the thing, and that's the last I remember. Thank heaven you're safe."

"I was winning, Saul," Diana said quietly. "I was just starting to get the better of that monster when you and Kirby came in. That broke the spell and I lost whatever edge I had."

"We only wanted to help you," Julian said.

Diana squeezed his hand. "I know."

She helped Julian to his feet. They peered around in the gloom.

"But where *is* Kirby?" Diana said.

They both looked down at Harriet's used-up body, then at each other.

"God, no, not Kirby," Diana said.

"It might not have happened," Julian said. "He might have got away."

"Kirby wouldn't have run. I know he wouldn't."

"We can't be sure," Julian persisted.

"Don't try to soften it for me," Diana said. "The demon took him. This is the way it happens, the demon leaves one body dead, like Harriet now, and it goes into the next person."

After all her steely self-control, Diana's nerves cracked for a moment and her shoulders jerked in a great wracking sob.

"I think I loved him, Saul. I never had a chance to tell him."

The little psychic put his arms awkwardly around her. "I'm sorry, Diana. I know it hurts, but we have to get out of here now. We still have your little boy to think about."

Diana pulled away from him, swallowing her sobs. "Yes, of course, there's Matt. How will we ever find him, Saul?"

"We have the power, remember? Between the two of us, with our minds locked on the same target, maybe we can reach him."

"Oh, yes," Diana said, "let's try it." She looked around the room of death. "But not down here."

Together they climbed the steps out of the basement and left the house. Back down on the cliff road, standing in front of Saul's little MG, they stood for a moment facing each other. Saul held out his hands and Diana took hold of them.

"Close your eyes," he said. "Concentrate with every ounce of energy you have on reaching your son. I'll do the same."

"Oh, Saul, what if it doesn't work?"

"It *will* work," he said. "Believe."

"Yes. Yes, it will work." Diana closed her eyes and squeezed hard the small hands of the psychic. She could feel the energy flowing into her as he answered her pressure.

She erased all other thoughts and formed a picture of Matthew in her mind. Silently she called out to him.

Matt . . . Matt . . . Matt! Hear me. Tell me where you are, Matthew. Tell me how I can find you.

Diana could feel the pulse throbbing in her temples as she concentrated.

Matthew . . . answer me.

Mommy!

The childish voice in her head was faint, but unmistakably Matthew's. He had not called her Mommy for a long time. Not unless he was hurt or badly frightened. Perspiration dampened Diana's forehead as she focused her mind on the small voice.

Tell me where you are.

Mommy! The water!

Where, Matthew? Where?

Here, Mommy. In the water by the rocks. I'm here. Under the crooked tree.

Diana's eyes snapped open. Saul Julian, his face just inches away from hers, still frowned in concentration. She pulled one of her hands free and turned to look along the cliff road. Standing stark and black against the moon, a quarter of a mile away, was a single twisted cypress tree that had withstood the ravages of the sea to cling tenaciously to the cliff.

"There, Saul," she said. "Matt's in the water down below that tree."

Julian did not hesitate. "Come on, we'll take my car."

They jumped into the MG and sped away from the old house toward the twisted cypress tree.

Diana leaped out of the car before it came to a full stop. She ran to the edge of the cliff, just beyond the tree, and peered down into the watery darkness below.

Julian ran up beside her, bringing a flashlight. He snapped it on and played the beam over the jumble of black rocks in the surf some thirty feet below. The

208

incoming waves, although they were not high, boiled and foamed among the boulders. The tide was coming in.

Diana heard it then, not in her mind, but for real this time—the sound of her little boy crying. She could sense his presence there below them, and leaned forward impatiently as the circle of light moved among the rocks.

Then with sudden clarity she saw him. She grasped Saul's wrist to steady the flashlight. In the water at the bottom of the cliff a long piece of driftwood, the broken mast of some wrecked sailboat, had become wedged tightly between two of the boulders so it pointed up at them like a warning finger. Lashed to the broken mast with his hands bound behind him was Matthew. Only the little boy's head was still above the water. The waves were already breaking in his face. His cries were weakening. In a very few minutes the sea would be over his head.

28

Slowly, painfully, Kirby Franklin's senses returned
The pains registered on his consciousness one by one
There was an ankle that seemed to be sprained, ar
abrasion on his knee that bled through a tear in hi
pants, a dull ache in his stomach, fiery pangs in hi
ribcage, and worst of all his head, which felt as if it had
been kicked into a potato shape. He heard a drawn-ou
groan, and was mildly surprised to realize it was hi
own voice.

With an effort he sat up in the darkness and banged
his tender head on something very hard. When the
wave of dizziness subsided he felt around the hard sur
face with his fingers and found it to be the underside
of a metal sink. The kind found in a laundry room. Ir
a basement.

His memory returned with a rush, the images of this
evening flashing across the screen of his mind in quick
cuts.

He remembered running down the stairs with Sau
Julian, past the cold furnace, and into another room
where Diana was locked in some kind of deadly struggle
with Harriet Nagle. Only it wasn't Harriet Nagle, bu
some unspeakable thing that wore Harriet's body and
a distorted mask of her face.

He remembered Diana turning to look at them, and the terrible roar that had come from Harriet's mouth.

He had run at Harriet with Julian right behind him. The creature had flicked out a hand with no apparent effort and knocked him to his knees. He struggled back up and was moving in to help Julian when a backhanded blow sent him spinning across the room to crash against the door to the laundry room.

Diana lay on the floor in a faint, and as Kirby struggled to get his limbs working again he had to watch helplessly the obscenity that followed. Harriet Nagle, or whatever was living inside her, squatted over the fallen Saul Julian and manipulated him into an act of brutally perverted sex.

As the heaving climax came, the life drained out of Harriet Nagle's body and she toppled awkwardly to one side. After a minute Saul Julian got slowly to his feet. His face was composed, but different now. There was in it the shadow of the fiend that had lived moments ago in the body of Harriet Nagle. Julian glanced down at the unconscious Diana, then over at Kirby. He smiled.

In the next few seconds Kirby Franklin knew a terror colder and deeper than anything in his experience. He realized that he was going to be the next victim of the demon's vile sexual transference. Julian, small of stature as he was, seemed to loom over him like Goliath. Kirby could not move, his muscles limp and useless. For just a moment he knew the terrible helpless rage of the rape victim.

As Julian began to lean over Kirby something stirred behind him. He spun around to see Diana beginning to wake up, then turned back to Kirby, eyes glowing angrily. Kirby never saw the kick coming. There was the explosion in his head, and the world had

burst apart in fiery fragments spinning into an endles
black void.

Now as he sat gingerly touching the bruise on th
side of his head, Kirby realized he had been spared th
ultimate humiliation of the demon's caress. He stag
gered to his feet, holding the edge of the laundry sink
for support. When his head cleared sufficiently, h
lurched forward, found the door, and kicked it open.

He was back in the paneled recreation room, from
where the demon must have dragged him. Only on
body lay on the floor there. Harriet Nagle. The dea
woman's flesh seemed to have collapsed in on itself, bu
the ravaged face was at rest. The demon had moved on
from Harriet to Saul Julian, and from Julian to—

In sudden alarm Kirby whirled, peering into th
shadows in all the corners. He saw no one, living o
dead. Diana must have left the room with Saul. Or wit
the thing that possessed Saul's body. Wherever Diana
was now, she would need help badly. If it was not al
ready too late.

Forgetting his injuries, Kirby stumbled up th
stairs, through the old house, and out the front door.

He stood for a moment at the top of the steps leading
down to the road and let the cold wind off the ocean
clear his brain. There would be nothing gained by rush
ing off blindly into the night with no idea of where
Diana and Julian might be. Kirby massaged his head
as despair welled into his throat. Then he saw the ligh
moving up the cliff road. Squinting toward the light he
saw the dull gleam of the white MG under the moon.

Kirby bounded down the steps and took off in a lop
ing run toward the light.

29

"There he is!" Diana cried. "There's Matt down in the water!" She turned to Saul Julian and gave him a smile of vast relief.

Julian looked over the edge of the cliff, then turned to answer her smile. "His head is still above the water level. We got here in time."

"Without you I could never have found him, Saul. If there is ever any way I can repay you..."

"Let's don't talk about that now," said Julian.

Diana returned her attention to the breaking surf below them. "You're right. The important thing is to get Matt out of there."

"I've got a coil of rope in the car," Julian said. "You wait here while I run back and get it."

"I don't think we'll need it," Diana said. "There's a trail over there that seems to lead down to the water. It's narrow but passable."

Julian shined the light over where she was pointing and picked out a rocky path that descended to the bottom of the cliff.

"I'll lead the way with the light," he said. "You stay close behind me."

Diana reached out to take his hand.

"Stop!"

Diana froze at the sound of the familiar voice. She turned slowly to see the tall, loose-jointed figure of Kirby Franklin running toward them along the road.

"It's Kirby," she said.

"Go on down to the water," Julian told her. "I'll hold him off."

"You can't handle him, not with the demon in him. You saw what Harriet was like."

"Go on," Julian said urgently. "Go to your little boy. I can take care of myself."

Diana took a tentative step toward the trail. Kirby was closing the distance between them in long, powerful strides. Saul kept urging her on, while down in the water little Matthew's cries were growing weaker.

"Get away from him, Diana!" Kirby shouted. He left the road and cut across the bluff toward them. "That's not Saul. It's the demon."

"Don't listen to him," Julian said. "He's the one the demon took. Not me."

Diana stood at the edge of the cliff in an agony of indecision. She looked from one of them to the other. Which was the man, and which the demon?

Kirby jogged to a stop six feet away. "You've got to believe me, Diana. He knocked me out and dragged me into another room in the basement. Don't let him touch you."

"He's lying," said Julian. "Get away while you can before he comes any closer."

"His eyes," Kirby said suddenly. "Look at his eyes."

Diana turned toward Saul Julian. All around the irises the eyes of the little psychic glowed a dull, sullen red.

"You're the one!" she said.

"Yes, Diana, I am Astragoth." It was no longer the soft voice of Saul Julian, but the ragged growl of the

214

emon. His hand shot out, the fingers clamped onto her arm above the elbow.

Held fast, Diana looked down again to the rocks where Matthew was lashed to the driftwood mast. The boy's face, pale in the moonlight, was turned up toward them. Diana could not be sure if he saw her. She tried to wrench her arm free, but the fingers, talons now, of the demon gripped harder, bruising the flesh.

Kirby Franklin clenched his fists and took a step toward them.

"Stay back!" Diana warned. "You can't fight him, Kirby."

"Good advice," said the demon. "Now I make my offer for the last time—give yourself to me as a bride should, or watch your little boy die slowly in the sea."

With a sudden effort Diana jerked her arm free. "You cannot defeat me, Astragoth. I know that now. Your power is not enough."

"No, I cannot take you by force," rumbled the demon voice. "But I can prevent you from saving the boy. You do not believe me? Then try to go to him."

Diana turned at once and took a step toward the path leading downward. A blast of fiery wind hit her like a fist, driving her back. She squared her shoulders and started forward again, and again the scorching wind stopped her.

The laughter of the demon boomed over the sound of the surf below.

"Mommy!" Matthew's voice carried up to her clear and very frightened.

"Matt!" Diana cried in answer. "Hold on, Matt, I'm coming."

"Mommy! The water! I—" The rest was lost in a strangled cough.

Looking down, Diana saw the wave break over her

215

son's terrified face. When the water receded Matthew's head hung forward, his chin resting on his chest.

"It is your choice," said Astragoth through the mouth of Saul Julian, "whether the boy lives or dies."

"Mommy, please help me."

For a third time Diana tried to start down the path but still she could not withstand the searing wind. The strength seemed to drain from her body, and she turned to face the demon. Everything was driven from her mind except the peril of her little boy. His life was worth any sacrifice she had to make.

The face that had been Saul Julian's stretched into an unholy grin of triumph. The eyes of the demon glowed cherry red.

Diana's head bowed in defeat. She sank to her knees.

30

Kneeling on the hard, rocky soil with her eyes closed, Diana felt the approach of the demon. The noxious odor made her want to retch. Her mind sought some small solace in this last desperate moment.

Diana had never been a religious person, so there was no personal god she could pray to for deliverance. She prayed instead to anyone who might hear that Matthew would survive, and that whatever must happen to her be over as swiftly as possible.

Something touched her shoulder, something cold and wet. The flesh prickled over her entire body.

"My bride," growled the demon voice. "My wait has been long."

Diana felt something probe under her clothing. Her stomach lurched.

"Diana, for God's sake, don't do it!"

She had a moment of confusion before she placed Kirby's voice. In her overriding concern for Matthew, she had forgotten he was there. She raised her head.

Kirby came running toward them. The demon stepped back from Diana and turned to face him with a bellow of rage. Kirby did not falter as he came on.

"Get away from her, hellhound!" he cried.

Diana struggled to her feet. At the bottom of the cliff

she could see that Matthew's face was still above the water.

"Fool!" the demon thundered at Kirby. "No mortal can challenge Astragoth."

The demon thrust Saul Julian's arms out before him, the fingers rigid and clawlike. A sharp crack of static electricity split the air. Kirby was lifted off his feet and hurled to the ground like a broken toy. For a moment he lay motionless, then groaned and struggled to his knees. He shook his head like a stunned boxer, then pulled himself to his feet and came on again.

The demon braced himself. The compact body of Saul Julian seemed to expand as he raised both arms to summon all the deadly powers of hell.

"Stop!" Diana cried, her voice ringing with command.

For a moment the scene was a frozen diorama. Kirby stopped in mid-charge. The demon, arms still upraised, hesitated, then turned to face Diana.

She looked past him to Kirby. "Matt is down below in the water. He's tied there in the rocks. Use the trail and go to him."

"What about you?" Kirby said. "And this devil?"

"I'll take care of him," Diana said. "It has to be me. Please hurry to Matthew. He needs you."

Kirby hesitated a moment longer, looking from one to the other, then ran past them and dropped from sight down the path that lead to the water.

Diana then turned her full attention to the demon. The body of Saul Julian blurred, wavered, and vanished. At last Diana faced the real Astragoth in all his festering ugliness. She did not flinch.

From the misshapen maw that was the demon's mouth came a bellow that blasted the night silence.

Diana stood her ground. "Powerful as you are, Astragoth, I am stronger."

With an effort that made the veins stand out at her temples, Diana willed into her body and her mind all the psychic force that she had denied in the past. She felt the strength entering her, coursing through her blood, nourishing her flesh. The power.

"No!" thundered the demon. "You belong to me!"

"I belong to no one. You have no claim on me."

The demon thrust toward her face an arm like a wet snake. The talons were crusted with filth. "Back, woman!"

The hot blast of wind hit her full on, but its force was diminished, the heat not so devastating. Instead of giving way to the demon, Diana moved forward.

From the bottom of the cliff Kirby shouted, "I've got him, Diana. Matt's all right."

She breathed deeply of the sweet sea air, and took another step toward the demon. Another.

"You are finished now, Astragoth."

"Never! No mortal can stand against me. There can be no end until I claim my bride."

"You have no bride. Return to the hell that spawned you."

The power surged through her body. The night air between the woman and the demon crackled with the cosmic forces set free by their battle.

Diana was invincible. She felt it. She saw it in the hesitation of the demon.

"Burn, Astragoth!" she commanded.

"No-o-o-o!" The demon's rumbling growl rose to an agonized howl.

The towering form of Astragoth seemed to shrink in on itself until once again Diana faced only the diminutive Saul Julian.

"Be damned, woman," he said in a weakening voice.

"Not I, Astragoth. It is you who will return to hell. Burn, demon!"

With a mighty *whomp* the body of Saul Julian burst into flame. The creature within him howled and beat at the blazing clothes. The face that leered out of the fire at Diana was a grotesque mask of rage and pain.

"To hell, Astragoth!" Diana cried. "To hell and be damned!"

The charred bits of clothing fell away and flames licked over the naked flesh of Julian's body. The angry red eyes looked one last time into Diana's, then Saul Julian, flames still crackling around him, turned and fled toward the sleeping town of Tranquilo Beach.

Diana started to follow, but stopped when she heard the voice of her little boy.

"Mommy!"

She turned toward the cliff and saw Kirby emerge at the top of the path with a soaking wet Matthew in his arms. She looked back along the lip of the cliff, where the burning man was now a distant torch as he ran away from them at incredible speed. From off toward the town came the bray of a siren.

Kirby set the boy down gently on his feet, and he stumbled into the outstretched arms of his mother.

Diana enveloped the boy and lifted him off the ground. The chilled wetness of his clothes soaked through her own, but all Diana could feel was the warmth of his living body and the beating of his heart.

"The water was getting higher and higher, Mom," he said, more excited than frightened now. "Kirby came right down the side of the cliff and saved me. Just like on *CHiPs!*"

"Yes, darling, you're safe now." Diana looked over her shoulder. Saul Julian was no longer in sight.

Kirby came over to stand beside them. "What happened to the . . . to Saul?"

"He broke away and headed for the town before I could finish him. We've got to go after him."

"What about Matt?"

"I'll hold him in my lap if you can drive Saul's car."

"I can drive it," Kirby said. "Let's go."

Diana wrapped her light coat around the boy and they piled into the MG. Kirby fired the engine and they raced back toward Tranquilo Beach.

"How do we know what to look for?" Kirby asked.

Diana glanced at him, watching for a reaction. "We're looking for a man on fire."

Kirby merely nodded and drove faster.

31

At the end of the cliff road an oncoming car slewed sideways in front of them, blocking the path of the MG. Kirby jumped on the brakes, swearing at the other driver as the sports car skidded to a stop.

A spotlight hit them in the eyes. Chief Ratcher ran over from the other car.

"Oh, Kirby, it's you. And Mrs. Cross. I had a call about some kind of disturbance on the cliff road."

"The boy had an accident." Kirby said.

"Is he all right?"

"We think so," Diana said, "but he should be looked at by a doctor."

"Want me to run him in to the hospital? He looks kind of cold in that open car."

"Would you like that, Matt?" Diana asked. "A ride in a police car?"

"Wow, yeah!" The boy grew serious for a moment. "Are you and Kirby going after the burning man?"

"Never mind about that," Diana said quickly. "We'll see you in a little while."

The transfer was made, and Kirby drove the MG on into town. Heading up the main street, they saw a knot of people standing outside the Red Snapper Grill. They

222

were looking toward the center of town, pointing and talking excitedly.

Kirby pulled over and shouted, "What happened?"

The bartender from the Red Snapper recognized him and came over to the car. "Somebody said it was a man on fire running down the street like the devil was after him. Me, I saw something going like hell, but I ain't ready to claim it was a burning man."

Kirby drove on. It was not hard to follow the demon's trail. Little clusters of people stood on the sidewalk staring in disbelief toward the far end of the street.

Kirby drove on to where the street ended at the park. Inside flashlights bobbed among the sound of excited voices and running feet.

"Oh my God," Diana said, "he's in there. In the park with all those little girls."

She and Kirby jumped out of the car and ran across the grass to where a thin woman with glasses was trying to calm several agitated Girl Scouts.

"What is it?" Kirby asked her. "What's the trouble here?"

The woman looked at him suspiciously. "Who are you?"

The girls, dressed in a variety of nightwear, clustered around them. Some of the girls talked with too much animation, others stared fearfully into the dark.

"I'm Kirby Franklin. Editor of the newspaper here. Now please tell me what happened."

"Some of the girls say a man ran into the park," the woman said. "Imagine a thing like that happening in this quiet little town."

One of the girls, blond and plump, about fourteen, spoke up. "It wasn't just a man, Mrs. Timmons, he was sort of glowing like."

"Glowing nothing," another girl volunteered, "he

223

was on *fire*. He went right past my tent. It was really *weird!*"

"Now, girls, let's don't make more of this unsavory incident than it already is," Mrs. Timmons said.

"Which way did the man go?" Kirby asked the second girl.

She pointed. "He ran into that patch of trees. There's another bunch of girls camped over there."

Without waiting to hear more, Diana and Kirby ran across the spongy turf toward the clump of trees the girl had pointed out. There too the girls were out of their sleeping bags, wandering around, calling to each other.

Diana grasped Kirby's arm to slow him down. "He's close. Very close. Be careful, Kirby, we don't know how much strength he has left."

They walked carefully into the clump of evergreens. Within a few feet Diana stopped with a gasp as she barely missed stepping on the charred body of Saul Julian. The flesh was blackened and split, the lips burned away to leave a death's-head grin.

One of the girl's who had followed them into the trees turned away retching.

Kirby knelt and examined the still-smoking corpse. After a moment he rose and stood close to Diana.

"He's finished," Kirby said.

"Saul Julian is finished," Diana agreed. "As for Astragoth the demon, we can only hope he is gone too."

She and Kirby walked slowly back through the park. Diana looked around at the scores of girls and their adult leaders. They were hastily packing their equipment, anxious to get away from the nightmare. Did one of them, Diana wondered, look back at her with eyes that glowed a sullen red?